THE BOY WHO BUILT A ROCKET SHIP ... AND ANOTHER

GUY RIDDIHOUGH

First edition September 2025
Story Text Versions 1.63
ISBN 979-8-9874940-4-2 (Paperback)
ISBN 979-8-9874940-5-9 (eBook)

Cover Design: Guy Riddihough

For

Aiyana & Thiany

and

Timothy & Jackie Ann

The Glass Weaver's Tale and Other Stories
BY GUY RIDDIHOUGH

I was six when I first saw kittens drown.
Dan Taggart pitched them, 'the scraggy wee shits',
Into a bucket; a frail metal sound,

Soft paws scraping like mad. But their tiny din
Was soon soused. They were slung on the snout
Of the pump and the water pumped in.

'Sure, isn't it better for them now?' Dan said.
Like wet gloves they bobbed and shone till he sluiced
Them out on the dunghill, glossy and dead.

from
The Early Purges by Seamus Heaney
from "Opened Ground: Poems 1966-1996"
(with permission)

Foreword

"The Boy Who Built A Rocket Ship" and "The Day It Snowed Forever" are primarily narratives about the loss of childhood innocence.

The first is the story of a young boy who worships his older brother as a mechanical genius and wants to help him in his secret revolt against the authoritarian society they are trapped in. However, he gradually learns who his older brother really is, and what the motives for his rebellion really are, and how their mother and father have struggled to include the older boy, despite his past, as part of their family.

The second story is about an older boy who, with his younger brother, revels in a strange and increasingly catastrophic weather event — an interminable snowstorm brought on by the vagaries of climate change. With the snow rapidly burying the city they live in, he learns of the evil that adults unfettered from social norms are capable of, and what he must do to defend the lives of his family.

Both stories explore facets of the inevitable loss of childhood. Childhood is, after all, merely a brief, transitory phase to becoming an adult. (If so, why does it exist at all? See the Epilogue for a biological perspective on the purpose of childhood.) However, despite its relative brevity, it has a profound and indelible influence on us and who we become as adults.

Childhood is a time of exploration — of the physical and mental worlds each child inhabits. These worlds differ profoundly from the worlds adults moulded into. Childhood is full of an alchemy that operates under a strange and pervasive logic only children can experience: colors are brighter and shadows darker; flames are full of faces and figures; clouds are populated with people and places; a cardboard box is a myriad things, its contents destined to gather dust; dull lead becomes gleaming gold, and showy gold is transmuted to lusterless lead.

The rules that confine adults to the narrow paths of their lives do not yet restrict the worlds of imagination in which children live. Children roam a much broader, unfettered interior landscape, if less so an exterior landscape, at least, in the West, in these days of helicopter parenting. Of course, childhood is not all magic and wonder. It is also necessarily a time fraught with challenges, anxieties, and fears, many of which are amplified by the novelty of these challenges, anxieties, and fears, and by a child's more intense, more visceral experience of the world around them.

Time, for example, has a much greater significance for children: inevitably, it occupies a much greater portion of their lives because they have experienced so much less of its passage, compared to adults. It travels much more slowly for them (a day is twice as long for a ten-year-old as it is for someone of twenty) and has a granular quality and a vastness that can be overwhelming. To a child, years mark eons, teenagers seem enviably mature, adults endlessly enduring like the ancients, and old people...old people are of a different race entirely, strange smelling, wrinkled as prunes, and yet oddly childlike.

For myself, there were days in the winter holidays when I would leave our house early in the morning, with my parents and sisters still asleep, cozy and warm in their beds, to see what mysteries the surrounding countryside might have in store for me (the rusting skeleton of a tractor, a brook to dam, the skeleton of a fox). In the chilly drizzle, under lumpen grey skies that looked close enough to reach up and touch, it seemed like the day might last forever, if I didn't freeze first, even though I was wrapped up against the cold. At other times, among the trees in a sun-dappled wood, walking with a friend and searching for blackberries or hazelnuts or, indeed, anything wild-growing and edible, it would also seem that the day must last forever, until the shadows lengthened and real hunger forced us home for dinner. Worst of all were the interminable Sunday afternoons, when I could no longer pretend to ignore the unfinished school assignment that hung like a punishment over my head, robbing the day of the endless possibilities I had woken up to.

Space is also different for children. Trivially, children are smaller; therefore, the world appears to them bigger. Trees had to be climbed (why else did they exist?), many were shockingly tall, towering into the sky and, once amongst their boughs and clinging tightly to a high branch, looking down revealed the Earth far below, terrifyingly distant. (As an adult, I have experienced the reverse effect when returning to a childhood home. I had thought the house truly cavernous, a place so vast we could race along its various corridors, and careen up and down the stairs like whirling dervishes, only to discover that it was, in fact, a rather pokey, cramped, and confining place.)

However, the effect of size is not simply a matter of proportion; it is a more complex effect of perception. Although children might understand that the Earth is a spherical planet, with a diameter of so many thousands of miles, they see and experience little more than their immediate neighborhood, which, while not large from an adult perspective, constitutes the entire known world from the child's point of view, against which all other spaces are measured. The bike journey to a nearby park might seem like a veritable trek, the journey to a nearby town an endurance test, and visiting grandparents an impossibly long trip.

A child's perception of the world is also much granular than that of an adult. Children live closer to the fabric of commonplace, everyday things, and are more intimately aware of their touch, smell, and taste. They can access spaces that adults might not even realize exist for occupation. In my own case, the airing cupboard, where the insulated water heater warmed the linen and towels, offered a corner I could wiggle into, wedge myself between wall and cladding, cozy and content, and hidden for as long as I wanted and free of the tyranny of the adult world with its rules and restrictions.

For children, dreams can also be places where fears and fantasies are rehearsed. As a child, I would often dream of a desert island, where, hidden among the palm trees, I'd find a stash of coins — heavy silver half crowns, two-shilling florins as big as doubloons, many-sided thruppeny pieces, silver tanners usually hidden inside Christmas puddings, dark pennies as big as the palm of my hand — and, waking, would look around desperately and wonder where all the money had gone. On visits to my grandmother's house, I was consigned to a thin, narrow bedroom, the sliver of another once much larger room in their strange, cut-in-half house. Lying in the narrow bed, the sound of my parents' and grandparents' voices filtering up from below would send me to sleep and, at the same time, fill the house with ghosts of women in voluminous ballgowns and men with handlebar mustaches smoking pipes, while down in the basement lurked unnamed terrors that could only be held in check by the presence of my grandfather.

As one childish fear is conquered, so another raises its ugly head in a long chain of perceptual transformations that are capped by adolescence and the dramatic physical and mental transition that hails the more or less imminent arrival of adulthood.

———

These stories are also, of necessity, about parents, and how they interact with their children, for better or worse. Parents assume a gargantuan statue in the eyes of their children. These are the adults by whom children gauge all adults, and so have a profound influence on a child's worldview.

I have learnt, being a parent, that it is impossible to get this most important of adult tasks right. Not that I failed to get the right answer; it is that there isn't a right answer. Every child is unique, and has different wants and needs that cannot be known in advance, are difficult to discern in the present, and that change with time in equally unknowable ways.

This is both an excuse and an apology to my own children. But it is also a forgiveness to my parents, now that I know what it is like to be a parent. Of course, my parents didn't get my upbringing right. Sometimes intentionally, but often unintentionally, they instilled in me a whole series of behaviors and beliefs that form the core of my personality, for better or worse. Some I have spent the rest of my life trying to unlearn, others I embrace as a central part of my individuality. But, now, I understand it would have been unreasonable of me to expect otherwise.

Guy Riddihough
  July 2025
  Washington DC

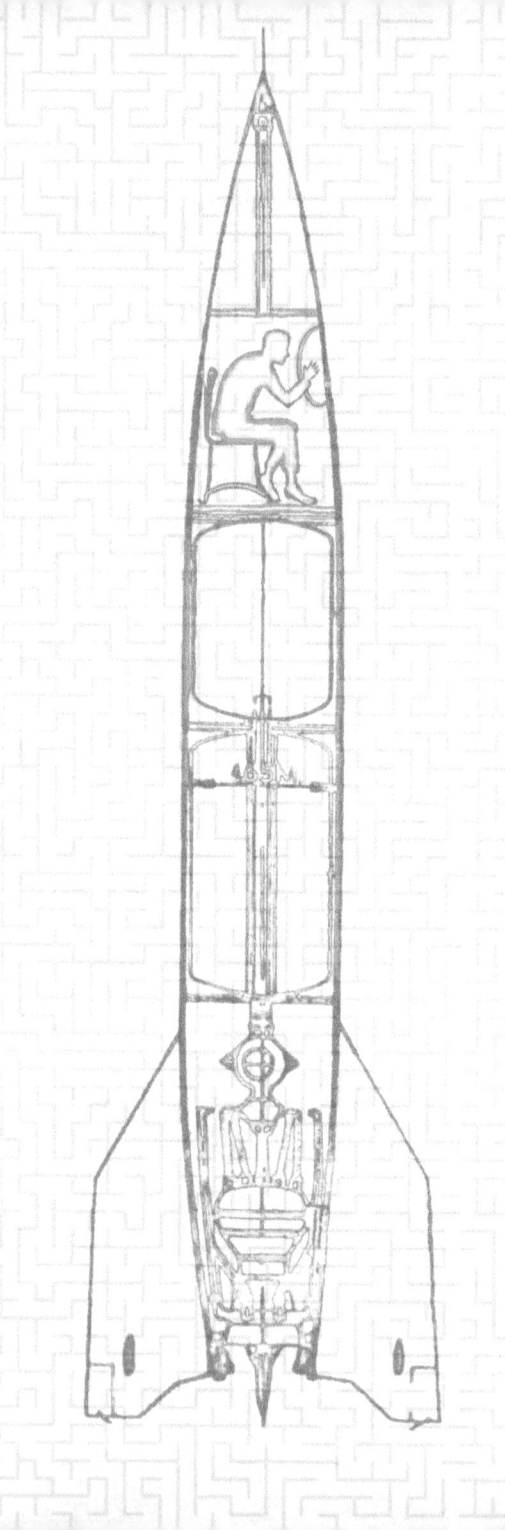

The Boy Who Built A
Rocket Ship

MY OLDER BROTHER Jim and I built a rocket ship.

He did most of the work: the hauling and welding, the cutting and caulking, the riveting and wiring, and all those other things needed to turn the shell of the derelict missile we'd found into a rocket that would fly.

Or, at least, we hoped it would fly.

I helped when Jim let me and where I could, and watched most of the rest of the time. There wasn't anywhere else I would rather be than helping him. I was sure my brother was a mechanical genius. I boasted to anyone who would listen that he could build anything — just you name it!

But I never once dared say anything about the rocket ship.

Because that rocket ship was a crime.

THE LAUNCH SITE was hidden in the ravine in the hills behind our house. It had to be. Right from the get-go, we knew full well that what we were doing was illegal. And there were informers everywhere, even among the other kids. Worse, I was pretty sure of the punishment we'd suffer at the hands of the militia if we got caught. We'd both seen what had happened in the township square to the man who had been called a saboteur. The Father Inquisitor, dressed in his ermine finery and purple robes, had been ruthless in the pursuit of justice.

I tried not to think about that. It didn't help my nerves, knowing Jim didn't care about the consequences, so single-minded was his determination.

I was not so sure.

From the very beginning, the rocket looked as fragile as an egg and, later, when it was full of fuel, as dangerous as a bomb. It smelled of oil and iron and was crooked in the middle, its stub nose pointing almost but not quite straight up at the great curve of the sky.

A sky filled with the beautiful, pockmarked face of Little Sister.

So, there was never any doubt about where he was planning to go.

"WHY D'YOU WANNA GO THERE?" I was on look-out duty, sitting on the ridge at the head of the ravine, keeping an eye on the surrounding countryside for informers and militia patrols when I first dared ask Jim: *Why d'you wanna go there?* Just like that.

And he never once told me the truth.

He had climbed up to join me, tired of working on the guts of the rocket for the moment, his hands covered in cuts and grease, and his fingernails all broken. He sat beside me on the big old flat rock up there, and, shoulder-to-shoulder, the two of us could survey the whole world.

We both looked up at Little Sister.

Little Sister's long, curved face was huge and green with summer, just like down here. Little Sister was close enough to see the glittering water in the crater lakes dotted all over its concave surface. But you couldn't see any of the people up there, not from down here, no matter how hard you squinted. Maybe with a telescope you could, but only the militia had access to telescopes.

Jim took a strand of grass out of his mouth and contemplated it. "Because things are better up there," he said. He didn't know, though. That was just his way of covering up the truth.

Do you want to know the truth?

Here's the truth: About a year ago, Dad had told Jim about his mom, his real mom. She was up there, on Little Sister. I remembered that night well. As soon as he knew, Jim made his mind up; he was going there to find her. But here's the thing: He never once said anything to me about what Dad had told him that night. And because of that, I could never ask.

He thought it was better up there? "That isn't what they say at school," I said, stung by his lie. The sharp pang of betrayal made me wince, and I had to look away momentarily. Why wouldn't he confide in me, his own, his only brother? He'd broken the sense of companionship I had felt just moments before. Now I wanted to goad him, hurt him back, challenge the whole crazy idea of the rocket ship. It wasn't only dangerous, it was illegal, stupid, outrageous.

Sly as a cat, he'd sensed the sudden change in my mood. "They don't want you to know the truth, *sprat*," he sneered. He only ever called me "sprat" when he wanted to put me down and remind me I was just a little kid.

Hurt, I shot back, "Everyone says they're evil up there, all the..." but I couldn't bring myself to say who they were — the words caught in my throat. "All the people who live up there on Little Sister," I ended lamely.

From where we sat, you could see the complete curve of the sky and the unbroken sweep of the valley below. Much of the land in the valley was tithed to our farm and cultivated, cropped, and grazed by Dad and Mom and the handful of itinerant workers they hired at various times during the season. Because of this, the farmhouse was all on its own at the foot of the ridge. The township further away, clustered around the bridge over the river. The sprawl of the city was far distant. The old cable rail station was off to the west, and the Supreme Council of National Unity's gray concrete fortress was to the east.

Behind us, in the ravine's shadow, we could just about glimpse the top of the rocket ship where the nose poked up through the trees.

Perhaps the sight of the fortress and its forbidding windowless walls made me want to impress upon Jim the insanity of this whole venture. I quoted one of the wilder rumors about Little Sister: "They eat their boy children," I said, clenching my fists. "That's what the older boys at school say."

Jim just laughed at that and narrowed his eyes to see the pock-marked but smiling face of Little Sister better against the long axis of the Sun. "You listen to those louts and their knucklehead cronies?" Nodding at the other place, he said, "I bet that's exactly what they say up there about us down here. That we treat each other like animals." He turned his gaze from Little Sister to the fortress. "Only they might be closer to the truth."

Saboteurs and traitors were taken to the fortress to be interrogated by the Father Inquisitor. Once you went in there, you didn't come out again. Unless they wanted a show trial, like those held in the township square every so often, to remind everyone what would happen if you turned against the Supreme Council. I was pretty sure that building a rocket ship to go to Little Sister made us both saboteurs *and* traitors. It was not a comfortable thought.

"You know what they'll do if they catch you building that

thing?" I said, but now my voice was quiet, and I was deadly serious, all the hurt transmuted into fear.

The sneer faded from Jim's lips, and his black eyes returned to the rocket ship. "You mean *us*, sprat. If they catch *us* building a rocket ship. Which means you don't breathe a word to no-one, ever, not even Dad if you value your spotty little hide." He turned his gaze on me, and it was hard and cold and made me shiver.

———

THE IDEA for the rocket ship was planted in Jim's imagination during the summer of the year before.

But the ground had to be prepared first before the idea could germinate.

It was late spring, and I was reading before lights out in my bedroom. I knew Jim was downstairs because Dad, standing at the bottom of the stairs, had called him down to the living room. This was usually the preliminary to a telling-off, and Lord knows we were always poking our noses into places and doing things that deserved a telling-off. But on this night, Dad's voice had an odd hesitancy that made me put aside my book, prick up my ears, and listen.

I could hear the low mumble of Dad's voice from the living room but nothing much else — he'd closed the door — so I kind of lost interest and returned to my book. A little while later, I became aware that the exchange had become more heated, and Mom was involved in whatever was happening.

I crept over to the bedroom door and put my ear to the keyhole. Dad was shouting. Jim was shouting back at him — something to do with Mom. Mom was trying to placate them both. I contemplated opening the door and sneaking down-stairs to understand better what was happening when there was the brittle crash of breaking glass. Jim was yelling at the top of his voice, and it sounded like he was thumping the walls. Something else went crash. I stood up, alarmed. Now Dad was yelling back at Jim, and Mom was shouting, too, trying to be heard over the din.

Jim had rowed with our parents before, for sure — he was easily offended and quick to anger, very unlike me — but this row was different: the hysterical shouting and, now, swearing; the sound of more things being thrown and broken; the exchange had become frightening in its violent intensity.

Shocked by all the noise, I retreated through my dormer window and onto the roof outside my little attic bedroom. I heard the living room door slam and the scuffle and grunt of a fight and Jim being smacked hard, once, twice, three times, and then the sobs of anger and humiliation that followed.

I sat still in the chill night air. I could hear Mom and Dad talking on the landing outside Jim's bedroom. He'd locked himself in and now was silent. A few minutes later, Dad came into my bedroom and, seeing it was empty, climbed onto the roof and sat beside me. He looked grim, his face flushed with exertion and the residue of hot anger. We sat in silence, watching the night sky, a sky dominated by the nighttime face of Little Sister.

After a while, he said, "It can be hard for Jimmy, sometimes."

I thought about this and then said, "What about me?"

Dad nodded, his lips pursed. "I know," he conceded. "And don't think I don't see how patient you have been with Jimmy and his moods." We looked at the little lights burning on the surface of the other place, most of them lights from windows of all the houses up there, many more than down here.

"I need to tell you something about Jimmy. It has been my responsibility to tell him for some time now, something which perhaps I should have told him sooner." He took a deep breath. I bit my lip, not knowing what to expect, expecting something fearful. "Mom is your mom, your real mom," he said. "She gave birth to you here, in this very house. But Mom is not Jimmy's real mom. Jimmy's real mom, his biological mom, lives up there, on Little Sister."

I frowned at this revelation. "Was that what all the noise was about?"

Dad nodded.

I thought about this for a long minute. "So, Jim isn't really my brother, then?"

Dad shook his head. "He most definitely *is* your brother, Joshua. Unquestionably. In the same way you are our son, Jimmy is, too. As far as we are concerned, there's no distinguishing between you."

I was chastened by the sudden intensity in Dad's voice and stayed silent for a while. I could see the tension in his face and knew he had more to say. I asked, "Why did Jim's mom, his other mom," I added, "give him to us?"

Dad's expression hovered somewhere between a frown and an odd, unfocused anger. "She was not allowed to keep him," he said.

"Why not?"

"Because...because no men and boys are allowed on Little Sister."

I looked up at Little Sister in surprise. I had heard the gossip that there were no men on Little Sister, but boys, too? The Supreme Council only ever referred to the inhabitants of "that place" as the *enemy*.

"There are no boys up there? At all?"

Little Sister looked like a boy's paradise to me: all those forests and hills and lakes and rivers to explore. Then I suffered a moment of horror: Perhaps the rumors whispered in the playground at school were true, and they did eat their boy children as soon as they were born, after all.

Dad shook his head. "When a baby boy is born there, he is sent here and either given to a family who will care for him, like us, or, more likely, entered into one of the boys' communes. That is the agreement between Little Sister and the Supreme Council of National Unity."

"That's terrible," I said, unsure if it was or not. Most of the boys at school came from one or other of the local boys' communes. The commune boys hated boys like Jim and me, who lived in families. There were a lot of fights between the two groups at school and around the township. Luckily, Jim was big for his age, unlike me, and, despite the sibling rivalry between us, he never allowed me to be picked on by the 'louts and knuckleheads' from the commune, and they dared not pick on him.

Now, I understood why Jim had gotten so mad and gone half-crazy.

Dad had just told him he was no better than the louts and knuckleheads from the commune we fought with and hated so much.

AFTER THAT, Jim retreated into himself.

He didn't want me around anymore. I didn't know what to do. I wanted to tell him that this thing about his real mother didn't matter, but it was not a subject that could be spoken of between us: I could not raise the matter, and he would not.

When he wasn't doing farm chores, he spent the rest of the time in his bedroom or tramping around the hills behind our house. Sometimes, when I persisted in following him, despite his admonitions to get lost, I'd catch him staring up at Little Sister, his eyes hooded and a strange, watchful look on his face. He hardly spoke when Mom and Dad were around. At school, he started goading the commune boys, getting into violent playground confrontations with them, and sometimes, if there was a large enough gang of them, coming off worse.

Mom and Dad saw what was going on. They went to the

school, talked to the teachers. It was no good. Jim flunked all his exams.

Dad didn't give up. He kept trying to bring Jim back into the family.

One day early in the summer holidays, he took a day off farm work and cycled with Jim and me out to the old ruined cable rail station.

And that's where it all started.

THE MASSIVE PYLONS of the station towered over the hills to the west, in a spinward direction, huge rusting sentinels pointing up at the looming face of Little Sister. We cycled along the long-deserted highway from the township, Jim in front, Dad in the rear, and me in the middle. We hid our bikes in the bushes when we got to the razor-wire-fringed fence surrounding the station.

The cable rail station was very definitely off-limits. That it was against militia law to prowl around inside doubled the thrill of exploring the place. The station had a semi-mythical status among the boys at school, and here we were, with Dad, about to go inside. My heart was in my mouth, and my eyes must have been as big as saucers.

Jim was cool about the expedition, shrugging nonchalantly when Dad told us we absolutely could not tell Mom what we were about to do.

We squeezed through a small rent in a section of the rusted chain-link fence, hidden behind thorny bushes far from the road. Inside, the buildings were deserted, windows broken, and doors boarded up. I was on tenterhooks, expecting militia soldiers to appear from around every corner. I kept my eyes peeled for their iron-gray uniforms and serrated knife insignia the whole time.

The rusting cable pylons arched into the sky, towering

over the cordoned-off complex. The huge, corroded cable drums, twice as high as a man and tipped over on their sides, were set further back, away from the buildings. Like the rest of the complex, they were slowly being enveloped by the encroaching wilderness, with bushes and shrubs even growing on the tops of the massive drums.

Dad took my hand, and we walked underneath a pylon. Jim scouted ahead, using a stick to scare lizards from their hiding places. The massive pylon arms and their cable guides were swept forward and up towards the face of Little Sister. Great coils of rusting cable lay strewn about the ground below, all around us, like the insides of some gigantic metallic monster.

"When I was a boy your age," Dad said, "the cable rail was still working." He squinted up at the rows of guide wheels for the cables on the pylon arms. "You could buy a ticket and travel on the cable rail to Little Sister. Only it wasn't called Little Sister then, of course. We called it the Uplands. The cable trains used to ply back and forth between here and there all day and night. I remember watching the lights glowing from the carriage windows as they made their way up and over to the other side, to spinwards, in the night."

We climbed up a tangled pile of cable and surveyed the mangled wreckage of one of the cable rail carriages. "This must have been one of the carriages that fell when the cable was cut. Dozens of people died, men and women, boys and girls."

"Girls?" I asked, surprised. "They came here?" Other than Mom, I knew of no other women. And I had never seen a girl, only ever in a few faded pictures in dusty old picture books.

Dad tilted his head to one side. "They didn't just come here, Joshua. In those days, men and women, and boys and girls, still lived together. And the Uplands, or Little Sister as we now call it, was a place anyone could visit."

We climbed through the wreckage of the carriage.

"All the people traveling in the carriages that fateful day fell to their deaths. It was terrible."

I looked everywhere, on the seats and the floor and piles of broken glass, but I didn't see any blood stains.

"And the falling cable, it uncoiled all the way back down here, killing even more people on the ground, too." Dad pointed ahead. "You can see it crushed those buildings there when it fell. Before that terrible day, there had never been an accident while the cable rail was in operation, though. Never once."

We climbed down the side of a mound of rusting cable and walked among more shattered and broken carriages.

I was still puzzled. "Why did they cut the cable if they knew people would die?"

"Because..." Dad frowned. "You have to understand this was a long time ago. The world was different then. The junta — the Supreme Council of National Unity — had taken over the government, supposedly to ensure our safety against saboteurs and terrorists." Dad sighed. "Ours is a precarious existence. It would not take much to end the world. Many people saw the junta's actions as a ruse by the military to take control of society. Where were all the saboteurs and terrorists? Most of those accused of sedition were opposition politicians, judges, lawyers, and captains of industry who dared object openly to the junta. They were put in prison or were 'disappeared.'"

I nodded, trying to look serious, and didn't ask what 'disappeared' meant.

"It was during the time of the disappearances that several prominent women came together and decided to leave. It was their way of protesting against the junta — the Supreme Council — and the strict martial law they had imposed. The wives of many of the disappeared also took to the cable rail with their daughters and, over time, made migrating to the

Uplands a statement of protest. Then, still other women followed them. That's how, over time, it became known as Little Sister. The name was kind of a joke at first. No one thought it would last for more than a few months or perhaps half a year or that nearly all the women would leave here and go there. It was just like that Greek play." He laughed and then became serious. "How wrong they were."

"Why didn't the Supreme Council make them come back before the women cut the cable?" Jim asked, standing nearby and leaning on his stick, watching Dad intently.

"No one knows who cut the cable. The junta says it was the terrorist sympathizers on Little Sister. But who knows if that is true? Especially after all this time. As to making them come back, well…" Dad started, then paused.

We had walked across the concrete base of the pylon and come to a long, low shed, newer-looking and undamaged, built after the cable fell.

Dad looked puzzled. "This wasn't part of the original cable rail station."

Then, the light of recognition came into his eyes. "No, this came later." He pointed at the shed. "That's your answer, Jimmy. This was where the junta — the Supreme Council — stored the missiles used to bombard Little Sister during the war. When the junta understood that the situation on Little Sister would not go away of its own accord, and once they realized what the consequences of this new circumstance could be, they threatened Little Sister with sanctions at first, and when that had no effect, with war."

I was shocked. "War? We fought a war with Little Sister?"

An apron of fire-blackened concrete stood at the far end of the long, low shed. A narrow-gauge rail track ran from the shed to the center of the apron, where a crane and a low, squat metal gantry stood.

"The junta declared the cable cutting and all the deaths that resulted as an act of war. The missiles they'd secretly been constructing and stock-piling were launched from there. They had been built before the cable was cut. You can still see the charring from the rocket exhaust," Dad pointed at the blackened concrete and then up at Little Sister, "and the damage the missiles caused. All those crater lakes. We are lucky the world is still intact and wasn't ruptured by the junta's bombardment."

I looked up at Little Sister's pockmarked face and marveled. "Those were all missiles?" I was impressed. The bombardment must have been something to see.

"The attacks only hardened the resolve of the women who had escaped to Little Sister and provoked even more to follow them by going overland and then making the perilous journey across one or other of the Lateral Seas." My gaze took in the two unremarkable quick-silver bands of water that defined our land's spinward and anti-spinward borders with those of Little Sister. "It was about then that the junta realized how perilous the nature of their position was. While the junta had the missiles, the women had something much more powerful: the ability to perpetuate our species because, of course, with few women remaining, there would be many fewer children born, and, over time, this place, our world, would end. The women in Little Sister were aware of this, too. There was a meeting between the two sides. A truce was declared, the junta agreed to cease the missile bombardment, and an arrangement was made, with men and women meeting on neutral territory, to ensure that children could still be born in sufficient numbers to maintain our civilization. However, the women declared they would never again allow even a single male, man or child, to remain on Little Sister. All would have to be returned to the Supreme Council of National Unity. And so it has been for all these years."

We clambered around the side of the shed until we found a door that had been prized half open. Dad squeezed through and I followed. The shed was dim and dusty and cluttered with moldering piles of scrap metal. Most of the missiles had been broken up.

"This was part of the truce agreement: Destruction of all the weapons used against Little Sister."

We crunched across the concrete floor.

In the far corner, we found one almost complete missile lying on its side on two narrow-gauge rail bogies, as if abandoned just before being wheeled out for launch. It was dented, with a bend in the middle, and the nose cone containing the warhead had been gutted and left empty, but much else—the shell, the fins, the motor, the fuel tanks, and the rocket nozzle—remained.

Jim examined the missile with an intense frown. Then he turned to Dad, demanding, "Why didn't Mom go with all the other women and girls?"

A half smile touched the corner of Dad's mouth. This was the first time Jim had called Mom "Mom" since the evening of the fight. "The cable was cut before all the women could leave. Mom was left behind. She did not want to risk the journey across either of the Lateral Seas. Later, after the truce was declared, she did not want to leave you and me behind. Which is lucky for us."

JIM WORKED HARD on the rocket ship all through that long, hot summer.

We both knew that the longer it took to complete, the greater chance there would be that we would be discovered. So, whenever he told Mom or Dad we were going out to play, he'd wait until no one was looking, head up the dusty path that led through the woods and into the hills behind our house, and work on the ship instead. And I'd trail along behind.

The rocket was tall enough that you could just about

make out the nose cone from the very top of our house if you climbed onto the roof and stood on the chimney pots or from the old cart track if you were looking toward the ravine. Most of the other commune kids were required to go to military training over the summer, and because the creek had dried up, one of the itinerant workers took the cow herd down to the much richer pasture by the river near the township. So, there was hardly anyone around. And with Mom and Dad working all hours of the day and night on planting, or the livestock, or the hundreds of other farm chores, it was possible to dismantle the abandoned missile, then smuggle it, section by section, from the cable rail station back to the ravine.

Jim got the material we needed to fix the rocket ship from anywhere he could, me tagging along to help — scrap from the smithy, old refrigerator parts from the dump, copper cable and rubber insulation from the trash bins outside the electrical generation plant, steering gear from the cable rail station, a wrecked steam car firebox at the wrecking yard. We stole stuff, too: plumbing supplies and a welding torch from the plumber, and even fuel from the fueling depot.

You might have thought it would be tricky to steal fuel, seeing as how dangerous that stuff was, but, in fact, it was easy. We just hung around the main yard in the liquified gas depot, watching the men working on filling up the cylinders with gas. Then, when they all went on their lunch break, we rolled one of the small cylinders out of the yard and through the hole in the back fence. We did the same for the spirit alcohol at the distillery, rolling a drum out through the publicans' entrance as if we were taking it to the owner of one of the gin shops.

No one connected the theft with us, a couple of prim and proper 'family' boys who went to one of the respectable schools in the township. We were just loafing around like boys do during the summer holidays — saboteurs were blamed, instead. One was even caught, and the theft of the welding torch, copper cable, liquified gas, and spirit alcohol was added to the list of crimes he was said to have committed.

They made a public show of his trial, holding it in the main square of the township. He was brought before the Supreme Council's Father Inquisitor and broke down under interrogation, admitting to our theft. Jim and me; we said nothing. We watched the torture and the public flogging that followed in silence while the other township residents jeered and shouted and scorned with malicious glee.

I was deeply affected by the trial.

It was the point at which I realized just how dangerous building the rocket was.

Later that day, after the crowd had dispersed, I went up to the place in the middle of the square where the saboteur had been manacled and hung by his wrists from the wooden flogging post. He was naked, tarred and feathered, branded with a branding iron, and bleeding from the flogging and the stones and bricks he had been pelted with afterward. Close up, I saw he had soiled himself, too, and that detail seemed to me of everything he had suffered the ultimate humiliation.

I wanted to apologize about the welding torch and copper cable and the fuel. He must have seen me standing there through his swollen, half-closed eyes because I heard him croak, "Water…thirsty…water…" I didn't have any water and was about to tell him when one of the militiamen saw me and, brandishing his gun, warned me away.

After that, the thought of getting caught kept me awake at night.

———

THERE HAD BEEN an explosion and a terrible fire a couple of years before at the gas liquefaction depot. Thirty-one men working there had burned to death. And here we were, using a piece of mesh hose and rusty cable clamps to connect the cylinder of gas and drum of alcohol/water mix to the engine via the turbo-pump.

The alcohol/water fuel drum sat below the warhead chamber, now the cockpit. Jim had welded one of the cable rail carriage chairs to the rocket frame above the drum. He'd strapped pillows to the chair and hung a makeshift parachute behind it.

"For easy access," he explained, sitting on the lip of the round port he'd bolted into the hole he'd cut into the side of the nose cone. I sat in the cable rail chair and played with the controls. Wires connected a joystick contraption to the rocket nozzle, which rested on gimbals, giving Jim a modicum of control over the ship's direction. There was no way to regulate the thrust and acceleration, though. Once the fuse was lit, the rocket would operate like a very large firework. We had stolen only one of the small liquified gas cylinders. Jim was certain it would help provide sufficient thrust to get him into the lower gravity region near the Sun's axis. Once there, his momentum should be enough to get him across to the other side of the world, where Little Sister's gravity would pull him back down to earth.

"What about the Sun?"

"I go at dawn when the Sun has not yet ignited at its edges."

"Why not go at night when the Sun is out?"

"At night? When the light from the rocket flare would be like a homing beacon for their militia? No, the Sun will help mask the launch."

"What happens when you get to the other side?"

"I unscrew the eight nuts that toggle the glass port cover in place, climb out with the chute, and jump." He twirled one of the brass butterfly nuts to show how. "Float down, lighter than a feather, and land with a gentle bump."

I thought about this. It sounded pretty flaky to me. "What

happens if there's an emergency? And the cross-threaded nut sticks?" pointing to the butterfly nut that kept getting stuck.

"Don't worry," he said nonchalantly. "I've practiced. I can get out in just under a minute."

I looked down at the fuel drum, the liquified gas cylinder, and the rocket motor, still visible through the unfinished bulk-head. If there were a fire, Jim would be cooked to a crisp in less than a minute. But I said nothing about that because I knew Jim was determined to go, regardless.

Instead, I said, "Do you think I could come, too?"

<hr>

TIME WAS RUNNING OUT.

Summer was turning into autumn. Wheat was turning to gold in the valley, and the first leaves were turning yellow on the trees in the ravine. The other kids, the commune louts and their knucklehead cousins, would return from their various militia training camps, and it would be impossible to conceal the rocket any longer.

The long, unstructured days of the holidays — when anything and everything seemed possible — were ending, too. School was due to start soon. I could already feel the constric-tion of lesson timetables, school bells, and the smell of chalk dust choking the life out of my imagination.

Worse, the wild magic of the rocket ship, so strong in the hazy summer heat, was slipping away. I was becoming more conscious of its myriad flaws, flaws we had put aside before: The cracked seams in the metal skin, the slow drip-dripping of the leak in the fuel line from the drum of spirit alcohol, the perished rubber of the engine gaskets, the uneven caulking in the bulkhead seals, the perceptible bend in the rocket's frame, the clumsily patched parachute in the cramped cabin, the cross-threaded butterfly nut on the nose port.

Was Jim really going to risk his life in this rickety contraption, propped up by wooden scaffolding and hidden in a ravine?

Would I do the same if he let me join him?

My burning anticipation for the launch was being eroded by the heightened sense of danger and a vague but growing dread of impending disaster. My dreams were filled with fire and flames, from which I was always running, running, struggling to open that brass porthole, the butterfly nuts too hot to whirl off their screws. I found myself half-hoping that he wouldn't be able to finish the rocket on time and that the launch would be stopped before it could be started.

I think Jim sensed this, too. The magic was fading and fading fast.

His frustration grew with every delay, with every technical difficulty, with every jury-rigged, duct-taped workaround. He would kick out at one of the four metal fins at the base of the rocket and the ship would ring with his anger.

But just when I thought it was all going to fail, just when Jim seemed like he was going to give up, somehow he got the rocket ship finished.

There it was. A short, stubby, oversized pencil, patched and welded, smeared with grease, and stinking of rocket fuel. All ready to go.

Jim looked at it long and hard, pursing his lips. My heart was in my mouth, expecting him to climb up into the cockpit and, for better or worse, set that rocket ship on its course. And in that moment, I realized I was ready to go with him, too.

Instead, he just turned away and walked home without a backward glance.

———

MOM HAD STARTED PESTERING us weeks before about the class assignments we were supposed to have done over the summer and whether we'd done them or not. Knowing that we hadn't, she had threatened a blanket moratorium on our going outside, other than for farm chores, until all the schoolwork was completed. Of course, we had been putting her off, making a show of pretending to work, but then slipping out to the ravine and the rocket ship as soon as she looked away.

That night, after Jim had turned his back on the fueled and ready-to-go rocket ship, Mom forced us both to confess to our wonton delinquency. Unable to explain what we had been doing instead of the homework, we were both grounded.

"You don't take another footstep outside this house until I have seen those assignments completed," she declared, red-faced with pent-up anger. Dad nodded in reluctant agreement.

"But Mom…!" I was horrified. Mom cut me off before I could start arguing.

"Not. Another. Word."

Jim didn't bat an eyelid. He got his exercise books from the cupboard and dusted them off as if the rocket ship no longer existed. He piled them on his desk in his bedroom and sharpened a bunch of pencils. Then, he sat down and started in on the long-forgotten remedial work for all the exams he had failed and would have to retake.

Mom looked pleased and triumphant. Dad was surprised and not a little suspicious. "Have you gotten a girlfriend or something, Jimmy?"

Jim just shook his head and frowned hard at the math problem he was struggling with.

I could not understand this sudden transformation. "Jim," I hissed, sitting on the window sill by his bed, giving him a meaningful look that could only be about one thing.

"I've got exams I need to retake, and you're disturbing me, Josh," was all he said, as if he meant it.

Could I concentrate on my homework? Of course, I couldn't. The only thing I could think about was the rocket ship, snug in its little glade in the ravine, behind the ridge, its stubby nose poking out from among the tree tops.

Its presence was both an unbearable taunt and a terrifying threat. There it was, all fueled up and just needing the fuse lit to send it up, up, up into the sky on the most thrilling, the craziest, most dangerous ride ever. And every moment it sat there waiting for us increased the chance that it would be found by someone else — the most incriminating evidence there could ever be against Jim and me.

I fretted all through the night. The first thing next morning, I climbed right to the very top of the roof, up onto the chimney stack, to see if I could still see the tip of the rocket ship among the trees. And…oh my Lord! I couldn't! My heart did a somersault and turned to ice in my chest. It had gone! I opened my mouth to cry out in pain. Instead, a cry came up from below. Mom had seen me standing on tip-toes on the chimney pots, craning right out over the sheer drop to the vegetable garden far below, and I was grounded twice over, not being allowed outside *or* into Jim's bedroom.

I tapped on the radiator pipes in my bedroom, trying to convey the disastrous news to Jim. There was no response. All that evening, I watched the track leading up to our house, waiting for a squad of militia soldiers to appear, rifles over their shoulders, serrated knife insignia on their uniforms, marching up the track to take us away to their windowless concrete fortress for crimes against the Supreme Council.

I waited and waited, staring through a chink in the window blinds, thoughts of my capture — the cold bite of the handcuffs, the forced march to the fortress, the jab of the gun barrel in my back — whirling around and around inside my head. I ached to tell Dad what we had done, to share the burden of my secret and lessen the loneliness and fear that wracked my soul, but I had made an unbreakable promise to Jim.

Hour after hour slid by and still they did not come. I

was exhausted, yet found it impossible to sleep. In the hour just before dawn, I convinced myself we had, by some miracle, gotten away with our crime. I slipped out of the window and onto the roof to let the night breeze cool my fevered brow. No sooner had I done so than I saw the movement on the track below I had been dreading all night. But it was not soldiers coming to the house, as I feared. Instead, it was a solitary figure, leaving the farm as silent as a mouse.

Jim.

There he was, dressed as dark as a monk, hurrying along the track into the hills. Was he running away? Leaving me behind?

I was after him in a shot, down off the roof, down the back stairs as light-footed as a cat, out through the downstairs bathroom window, running across the dewy grass of the back lawn and then full pelt along the path through the shadowy woods, petrified I would lose him in the dark. My shoes and the lower part of my trousers were soaked long before I caught up with him.

When I did, Jim didn't even turn to see who had followed him.

"You're not coming. You know that, *sprat?*" he said without looking back.

"Where?" I panted, out of breath.

He was following the path to the ravine.

"Jim," I said, tugging at his arm, "It's gone."

He laughed knowingly. "No, I hid it."

We marched up the track, into the ravine, and then the glade. He was right. There was the rocket, branches tied into a crown of leaves sitting on the nose cone.

I let my breath out, all that fear draining out of me like puss from a boil.

He said again, "You're not coming, do you understand?"

Is that why he had crept out on his own? Gone through

that whole charade of being disinterested? Just to get rid of me?

I smiled, holding the hurt inside. "I gotta light the fuse, though, right? And anyway, there's only one parachute," I said as if I had known all along that I'd not be going with him.

Jim said nothing and walked around the rocket ship like he was giving it one last inspection. Hands in pockets, he surveyed it from base to tip and then looked up, as if it were for the first time, at Little Sister, where she hung on the curve of the pre-dawn sky. It was too dark to see his expression. As we watched, the Sun ignited in the center of its span across the sky, heralding the dawn.

"Time to go," Jim said to himself. Then, to me, "OK. You can light the fuse. Like we practiced, remember? You crawl under the bell and light the taper. Then, you take the taper and reach up through the throat of the nozzle and into the combustion chamber, where the fuse is. Once the fuse is lit, you bang on the bell three times. One, two, three, like that." He demonstrated, using his fist on the side of the ship. It reverberated in time to his pounding. "I'll give you thirty seconds to get out of there before I open the stopcock on the fuel tank. So, once you are out from under the bell, you run like hell. Got it? I don't want you crisped. Imagine what your mom and dad would say."

I said, "Sure!" This smallest of concessions filled me with an irrational sense of relief — I was still in on his big secret, still part of the gang. But, I had heard that "your," too, and it burned. I didn't show even a twitch of an eyebrow, though. "As soon as it's lit, I'll watch the launch from the ditch."

"Yeah," Jim nodded. "Sure, whatever."

I just stood there, wondering whether to say goodbye. I suppose I still couldn't believe he was going. Perhaps he couldn't, either. I watched him climb up into that cramped cockpit in the nose cone, where the warhead had once been housed, and shut the port behind him, screwing down each of the eight butterfly nuts one at a time. I wanted to shout to him to tell him to leave the cross-threaded one open, just in case. But by then, it was too late.

So, my final part in this whole saga was to light the slow-burning fuse in the throat of the exhaust nozzle at the mouth of the combustion chamber, and I wasn't going to mess that up because I had promised Jim I would do it.

I squirmed under the rim of the bell, through the narrow gap between metal and ground. The cramped space inside the bell was dark and stank of rocket fuel. I set about lighting the taper using the gunflint Jim had stolen from the blacksmith. It took over a dozen clicks of the flint before I could get a decent enough stark to set the taper going. When it caught, it sputtered and flared, lighting up the ribbed wall of the bell, giving me a monstrous shadow that loomed over my shoulder, no matter which way I turned.

The wall of the bell curved up to the throat of the nozzle, over my head.

The fuse was up there, somewhere.

I reached up and jammed my arm and head into the constriction of the throat, using the lit taper to find the fuse.

Standing there, looking up into the combustion chamber, I could imagine what an autumn leaf blown into the mouth of the iron foundry's blast furnace must feel like.

Of course, the end of the fuse had to be behind my head, where I couldn't get at its end without having to extract myself from the constriction. As I wriggled free, I dropped the taper, which went out in the wet grass. It was the devil to light, and then I still had to squeeze back into the throat of the bell, the right way around this time, to get at the end of the fuse. I could hear Jim clambering about somewhere above. I prayed he had not gotten impatient and decided to open the stopcock on the fuel tank ahead of my signal.

My hand was trembling as I held up the taper.

Carefully, carefully…

Almost before I realized it, the fuse was lit and burning fast.

Bits of ash were falling on my face and into my eyes. I twisted and pulled myself out of the constriction, blinking and spitting, and pounded on the bell to let Jim know the fuse was lit. The bell boomed like one of the bells of doom.

As I crouched to escape from under the exhaust nozzle, I slipped on the wet grass and clanged my head against its metal rim. The blow stunned me for a moment, and I sat staring at the gap between the rim of the bell and the ground. Then I was down on my belly and shoving my way out through the gap into the light and fresh air. I scrambled to my feet and scampered away from the rocket. But I didn't run straight for the ditch. Instead, I stopped and turned to look back.

I waved up to the circular port in the ship's nose and mouthed, "The fuse is lit!" as if, by some chance, he had not heard my fists beating against the inside of the bell or my head hitting it as I slipped over.

Was that Jim waving back? My heart leaped! Had he changed his mind about me coming with him and was beckoning to me?

The reflection of the pre-dawn sky in the glass obscured my view. I hesitated, not sure what to do. Go forward, backward?

The rocket engine coughed, belching out a great cloud of hot black smoke, reeking of fuel.

That was all the signal I needed.

I turned and tore for the ditch.

Behind me, I could hear the roar of the rocket motor starting up. Glancing back for an instant, I saw a brilliant jet of flame shooting out from the bottom of the rocket. Its radiant heat seared my face. I threw myself into the ditch, landing splat in the muddy water at the bottom.

An enormous roll of thunder hammered at the air. Scolding rocket exhaust billowed all around me, enveloping me in its powerful chemical reek. I jammed my fingers into my ears and thrust my face into the water.

After what seemed like an age when I felt sure I was about to suffocate and drown, I gave in, raised my head, and breathed in the foul, smoky air in great choking gulps.

Looking up through the smoke and the trees, I could see the brilliant light of the exhaust flare rising into the sky. Would there be enough alcohol and liquified gas to get the ship across the Sun's axis before the Sun was fully ignited? The skin on my face and hands tingled as I watched the diminishing jet of flame veer to the left of the partially ignited Sun. Then the rocket motor cut, as the fuel ran out. Still, the trail of smoke and condensation rose higher and higher, crossing the axis of the Sun, and I was sure he'd made it.

I shouted with pure elation, my throat raw from the burning exhaust.

"We did it! We did it!"

Then, I broke into a fit of wheezing and coughing that almost killed me.

Once I had caught my breath again, I just knelt there, face upturned to the sky, smelling the smoke and stink of rocket fuel and feeling the cold water seep through my clothes to chill my skin, knowing we had managed the impossible. My temporary deafness faded. I heard the sound of the trees around the launch site crackling and burning, set alight by the great petal of flame that had blossomed from beneath the rocket as it rose into the sky.

Mom's voice, calling out, broke into my reverie of wonder.

She was shouting our names — "Joshua! Jimmy!" — over and over. I stood up, soaking and covered in mud, and scrambled out of the ditch.

Looking up through a break in the burning trees, I could

see the exhaust plume weaving drunkenly up towards the lustrous face of Little Sister. Jim was somewhere far beyond the end of that long tail of smoke.

Then Mom saw me and let out a scream. She ran over, whisked me into her arms, and hugged me as if she intended to break me in half.

"What happened to you?" She was wiping the mud and dirt from my face.

"I was watching the lift-off!" I said in a hoarse croak.

"Where is Jimmy?"

I looked at Mum. Looked away.

"Joshua. Look at me. Where is Jimmy?"

I looked down at the ground. Then up at the looming face of Little Sister, besmirched now by the dispersing exhaust plume.

Following my gaze, she pleaded, "No, Joshua. Don't tell me that was him." She shook me. "Joshua!"

Dad appeared out of the smoke. "I've called the bombardiers!" He saw me. "Good God, Josh. Look at you! You're as pink as a piglet and bald as a coot!"

I touched my face. It was burning hot and painful under my fingertips. I moved my hands over my head. It seemed like most of my hair had gone, burnt away by the flash of heat from the rocket motor.

"Jimmy's gone!" Mom said.

"Gone where?"

"Up there."

Dad stared up into the sky like he couldn't believe it.

Mum broke down into tears, sobbing, "No, no, no, no, no!" After a ragged pause for breath, she said, "I have to get him back! I don't care what I have to do! I don't care what it takes! Even if I have to go and get him myself!"

Then the bombardiers arrived.

THE BARBER HAD to shave my head to remove the tufts of hair left after the launch, so I really did end up clean bald. My head looked like the top of an odd, pink egg.

Word about Jim's flight went around the township like lightning. On the omnibus to school that first day of the autumn term the other kids snickered, and whispered, and pointed at me, with my bald head and bright pink face. I didn't care. I was so proud of Jim. He had built a rocket ship and flown it to Little Sister.

At least, I hoped and prayed he had.

Later on, on the night of the launch, after the bombardiers had put out the ring of burning trees around the launch site, and the doctor had checked me for burns and lung damage, and the Constable had taken down my story of what had happened, and I had been sent to bed by Dad, I climbed out on the roof and looked up at the vast glowing night-time face of Little Sister. The exhaust plume had long since blown away in the gentle breeze. Only the smell of the burnt trees in the ravine remained as a reminder of what had happened.

I wondered where Jim was. Somewhere up there. Little Sister was covered in clusters of lights, all those night-time towns and villages, all full of women and girls, no men and boys at all. Well, not no men or boys. One man. One boy.

Jim.

Hopefully, he'd have been able to dodge the militias and the constables and what all they must have up there and be able to hide out somewhere. Did they even have militias and constables there, I wondered. I had no idea. I was sure he'd try to signal me to let me know he'd made it OK. We both knew Morse code from school. I scanned Little Sister's face for a blinking light — dash-dash-dash, dash-dot-dash — but there was nothing.

Had they seen the exhaust plume coming up from here — or down, from their up-side-down perspective? The rocket flare should have been obscured by the Sun's ignition. But what about all the smoke? Once the fuel ran out and the motor cut, Jim would have pulled on the homemade parachute, made the jump, ditched the rocket ship, and left it to fall where it may, down onto the other side of the world. So, even though they'd find the crashed rocket, they shouldn't have found Jim. But there was a little icicle of fear in my heart. What would happen if he couldn't get the port open in time? I cursed those stupid butterfly nuts. He'd closed all eight of them, even the one with the crossed thread. What if that one had jammed? As the ship fell and gravity increased, it would have fallen faster and faster until…

I felt tears prickle in my eyes.

There was a noise behind me, and Dad was climbing out of the attic window. He sat beside me on the roof and looked up at Little Sister. I wiped the tears from my face. He didn't say anything for a while. We just sat side-by-side, looking up at the sky.

"Jimmy did a brave thing."

I didn't say anything; I kept looking up, trying not to cry.

"A brave and foolish thing, Josh. I know you must have helped him, and I respect the loyalty you showed him by keeping that rocket a secret. That must have been a big thing, a hard thing to do. But it was also a dangerous thing, Josh. We all love Jimmy and want him to be happy, but we also want him to be safe and sound."

In my mind's eye, I saw Jimmy struggling with the butterfly nuts on the port as Little Sister's gravity pulled the rocket further and further down. I was crying uncontrollably now. I couldn't help myself. Dad put his arms around me.

"He'll be OK, I know it. He's a tough kid like you. You're both tough kids and me and Mom love you more than anything in the world."

But another thought had occurred to me over those long

hours since the launch. The words, when they came, came out in a rush.

"What if Mom goes to Little Sister? To get Jim back. They would never let her leave again because she's a woman. She'll want to stay with him and never come back here!"

Dad hugged me closer. "Your Mom wants to stay here with us. She loves us very much and doesn't want to leave us. She wants Jim back here so we can be a family again." Dad's voice quivered, and I could feel a tremor inside him as if his heart was quaking at having to speak. "Jim's mother will have another family by now. She'll be with her new children, whom she'll love as much as we love you and Jimmy. Remember, Jimmy was only a tiny baby when we first brought him home. I am afraid Jimmy will only be a distant memory for her."

He, my Dad, was almost crying. I held him even tighter to reassure him I loved him with every fiber in my body. We embraced, silent, under the impassive face of Little Sister.

I had another fear. "But what if Jim wants to stay there?"

Dad had regained his composure. He shook his head, "There are no men, no boys, on Little Sister. Although it will be tough for Jimmy, I am sure they will not let him stay there. Mom is more worried about the junta — the Supreme Council — and what they will do to Jimmy when he is sent back from Little Sister."

I asked, in a small voice, "What about me?"

Dad gripped my hand, "Neither of you have anything to answer for."

Shame-faced, I said, "We stole things, Dad." There was a lump in my throat, making it difficult to speak. I swallowed. "We stole some of the things the Father Confessor said the saboteur had stolen. Jim and me." I thought of the saboteur in the square and felt myself grow cold and shivered. He had been left hanging there as a warning and died three days later of thirst.

Dad said, "That was nothing more than a show trial, Joshua. Everyone knows those charges were false. I am sure that poor man did nothing, nothing at all. No, his crime was being popular with the people and, therefore, a threat to the junta. Your boyish high jinks have nothing to do with what happened to him. I will tell you this — if the Supreme Council tries to lay even as much as a finger on you or Jim, they will have to face me first."

EVERY NIGHT, I watched the constellations of lights on Little Sister. Among all those lights, perhaps there was one blinking for me. But, as much as I looked, the only blinking seemed to be caused by clouds passing over Little Sister's face.

I was desperate for a sign, anything to know he was alright.

The whole situation left me as taut as a bowstring.

During those first days back at school, the other kids couldn't keep their eyes off me and my bald head, eyebrows gone, and face pink as a piglet.

In class, they whispered, "Was it the militia? Did they do that to your head?"

"They tar and feather you, like that saboteur?"

"Is it true that Jimmy tried to get to Little Sister?"

"He didn't try!" I snapped back. "He made it. He's there now. He sent a signal back," I lied.

"Joshua Lansdowne! Not—another—word!"

I ducked my head and kept my eyes on the textbook before me.

It seemed like everyone was looking at me, all the other kids, all the teachers, the whole school, the whole damn township! If I could have run away, I would have, but I was afraid it would kill Mom and Dad if I did, so I stayed for them.

During recess during the second week, a group of older

boys—commune louts—came over to the basketball court, where the younger kids hung out.

"Hey, egghead."

I pretended not to hear.

One of them came over and slapped me, hard, right on the top of my now fuzz-covered head. It stung.

"Hey, it *is* just like a hairy baby's bottom!" They roared with laughter.

"Big Jimmy ain't here to look after baby no more. Fried in that idiot tin can of his."

One of the others said, "Nah! Splat…on landing."

They started shoving me. The other smaller kids, sensing danger, edged away.

"He isn't dead," I said, desperately holding back the tears in my eyes.

"Ooh, baby's getting angry. Doesn't like it that Big Jimmy is tomato soup in a can."

"*Fuck* you!" I shouted.

They paused, taken aback by the potency of that forbidden word uttered within the bounds of the schoolyard.

But its dark magic did not last long. One of the louts shoved me again, trying to make me fall over. I staggered and then head-butted him on the chin — *crack* — and he pulled me down with him as he toppled over. Just what they wanted. They started kicking and punching, and I felt like I was fighting for my life, with no Jim to come and pull me free.

The cry went up around the playground, "Fight, fight, fight!" and kids thronged around us, making a tight circle, penning me in and trapping me with my enemies. I swung and kicked and bit and spat with all my might and knew from the swearing that I was making contact. But there were more of them than me, and they were bigger and stronger, and they were making contact, too.

The teacher on playground duty pulled us apart.

I was left dazed and bruised and bleeding from the beating, my ears ringing and my eyes blurred with tears of rage and humiliation. The massed spectators were dispersed, and the combatants were taken off to the principal's office.

Mom took one look at my face that night and wrapped me in her arms. Dad helped with the antiseptic cream and plasters. "Would you like to take tomorrow off?" he asked.

I pretended to think about it and then shook my head. I couldn't hide. That would be a sign of weakness, just what the commune louts would watch for. And I could not turn to Dad for support. I had to face up to them on my own — that was the unwritten lore of the playground.

Perhaps reading my thoughts, Dad nodded.

I sat on the attic roof that night, praying for a sign.

THE ARRIVAL I had dreaded from the beginning of the whole rocket-ship business happened a week later. It occurred before I was aware of what was going on. I had been weeding in the vegetable garden for Mom, and I swear there had been nothing on the track leading up to the house the moment before. And yet, when I looked up again, a shiny black car was rolling up to the front door, its tires crunching on the gravel.

Its windows were dark and impossible to see through. But I knew straight away who it contained. My bowels turned to ice.

Three militia soldiers got out, one of them carrying an ugly stub-nosed submachine gun. They were all dressed in their iron-gray uniforms with the serrated knife blade insignia on their shoulders. They fanned out around the car. Then, the Father Inquisitor stepped out. He wasn't wearing his official regalia, no ermine, and purple robes. Instead, he wore a dark suit, dark glasses, and black leather gloves. He looked around at the house and its surroundings. I hid between the rows of beans I had been clearing of pigweed before he could turn his head in my direction. Through the leaves, I saw he gave my hiding place a long, considered gaze. Then he adjusted the black leather portmanteau under his arm and signaled the militia soldiers to move to our front door.

As soon as they were out of sight, I ran into the house through the backdoor and waited, shivering, in the kitchen while the Father Inquisitor and two of the three militia soldiers were taken into the living room. Out of the kitchen window, I could see that the third soldier with the submachine gun had stationed himself at our front door, waiting for anyone who might dare approach the house.

Mom shooed me upstairs, and Dad closed the door to the living room. The men spent a long time in there, talking to Dad.

I sat on my bed, knowing they would come for me next. I thought about running away. But to where? I needed Jim. How badly I needed him.

Mom came up and told me the Father Inquisitor wanted to talk to me, too.

I had to will myself to control my trembling. Mom took my hand and gripped it hard. "There is nothing to worry about, Joshua, not while I am here."

Dad met me on the stairs.

"Josh, the Father Inquisitor wants to ask you a few questions." He held my arms. "Just tell him the truth."

I nodded, the serious look on his face making me feel even more afraid. The saboteur had not been cut down from the whipping post long after he had died, so the smell of his rotting corpse had filled the square. And when the wind blew from the south, we could smell it in the schoolyard.

Dad ushered me into the living room.

I looked back, "Dad? Aren't you coming in, too?" My voice quaked.

He smiled and shook his head. "I'll be just outside."

One of the soldiers nodded at Dad, and he left the room, closing the door behind him.

The two soldiers positioned themselves in front of each door, barring entrance or exit from the room. They watched me the whole time.

The Father Inquisitor sat in Dad's armchair, still wearing dark glasses and black gloves. I was petrified but also gripped with an insane urge to tell him to get right out of that chair. No one sat there except my Dad. I clamped my mouth shut and sat on the edge of the other armchair, my heart hammering in my chest.

"Hello, Joshua. Do you know who I am?"

I swallowed, paralyzed, unable to speak.

"Perhaps you remember me from the trial in the township square last year. Everyone was required to go." He leaned forward. "Did you go?"

I made the slightest motion of my head: Yes.

"Good," he said, considering me over his gloved finger-tips. "So, you will know that I need to ask you a number of questions about the — treasonous — event that happened here nine days ago."

I stared at the Father Inquisitor's shoes, terror mesmer-izing me. A babble of explanations, excuses, and admissions rose in my throat.

"Joshua, do you understand that what your brother did was wrong? Very wrong?"

I looked at the Father Inquisitor and his two silent companions. I nodded, still not daring to speak.

"And you didn't tell anyone? Even though you knew it was wrong." His voice was soft, and his tone was patient and reasonable. He spoke as if forming each word on his tongue before letting it out of his mouth.

"Jim asked me not to," I said, then clamped my mouth shut again.

"Why did he do that?"

"Because Dad would be mad."

"So, your father knew nothing of what you and your brother were doing?"

I shook my head.

"Do you think it strange he was able to build a rocket all by himself?"

I didn't say anything.

"You helped him build the rocket, didn't you?"

"Only getting stuff. I didn't build it. He wouldn't let me."

"That's convenient." He narrowed his eyes behind those dark glasses. "For you. Did your father tell you to say that?"

I shook my head again.

The Father Inquisitor sat back in Dad's chair. The steeple he had made of his hands gave him the attitude of someone at prayer. "You understand he can't have built the rocket all on his own, Joshua, now can he?"

I didn't say anything.

The Father Inquisitor's face did not change, but something inside him did. "Who helped him, Joshua?" I could tell he was angry, but he did not want to show it, not yet.

"Jimmy must have had help from someone else. Making a rocket ship is a complicated thing to do."

I shook my head again.

The two soldiers looked at each other where they stood in front of each door. The Father Inquisitor leaned forward towards me. "It was an adult, Joshua. An adult must have helped him. Who was it, Joshua?"

I looked from him to the two soldiers. "No," I said, "No one helped him. " I could see from the soldiers' faces that this was the wrong answer. I knew what they wanted me to say: Dad had helped him.

"But you didn't see him make all of it, did you? Perhaps someone helped him when you were not there."

"I didn't see anyone," I said. "Ever. Jim never mentioned anyone else, ever."

"You can't be sure, though, can you, Joshua? Someone might have helped and you didn't know about it." The Inquisitor made a little sound of pent-up exasperation. "Do you understand how important this is, Joshua? Do you understand that Little Sister intends to destroy us? All of us? Because without women, you and I, all of us, all men, would disappear. Do you understand that?"

"They send the boys born on Little Sister back here," I said as if this might somehow placate him.

"Yes, they do. But what happens if they stop doing so? What then?" His gaze behind those smoked lenses was fixed on me. "Or worse: what if they find a way to have babies without men and ensure all the babies born on Little Sister are girls? There would be no boys to return to our communes here to grow up into men, populate our world, and stand against Little Sister. If there were no boy babies, we, you and I, your father and brother, we would all grow old and die, and our world would come to an end. There would be no one, no *men* left. Now, do you see how easy it would be for them to be rid of us all? How tenuous our existence is? How dangerous the saboteurs, traitors, and fifth columnists are? Their misguided sense of 'morality,'" he laughed bitterly, "only weakens our civilization, something we cannot tolerate in the face of this greater threat."

I remained silent, my eyes defiant, his words passing through me, heard but unheard.

"We live teetering on a knife's edge, Joshua, in constant danger of slow annihilation by the tyranny that is Little Sister and undermined by conspirators among our own people. There is no room here for anyone — *anyone* — who would willingly collaborate with our sworn enemy. Now, for the last time, tell me, who helped your brother?"

DAD CAME from the kitchen as one of the soldiers ushered me from the living room. He squeezed my hand and smiled at me, and I could see in his eyes that he wanted to say something, but the soldier was right there, and he couldn't. Instead, he entered the living room, and the soldier closed the door behind him. Mom hugged me and sent me back to bed. I lay there, listening. I could hear the mumble of conversation from down below. What were they telling Dad, those militia soldiers, and the Father Inquisitor? It seemed to me they would be prepared to lie, telling him I had said he had helped us. They would force him into a confession to save Jim and me from the fate of the saboteur in the square. I tossed about between the sheets, falling into and out of this recurring nightmare.

An exclamation brought me bolt upright in bed.

The exchange downstairs had become heated. The Inquisitor was angry. I listened, straining to hear. The Father Inquisitor barked something, a command, and there was a quieter response from Dad. My whole attention was focused on the sounds from below, desperately trying to divine what was happening. Someone was striding across the floor; there were more barked words, a softer response, another exclamation, a pause, and the same exclamation repeated more emphatically.

My heart thumped in my chest. I was very afraid of these men. They were trying to frighten Dad the way they had frightened me. I was angry, too. I wanted to go down and stand by his side and tell them they couldn't make Dad or me lie about what had happened.

They left much later. I was awoken by the front door slamming shut. In an instant, I was out of bed and at the attic window, just in time to see the black car drive away into the night. The windows showed nothing of who was inside. Still, I strained to see until there was nothing left to see, fearing the nightmare had come true.

I had to suppress a violent urge to race after them along the track, beating on the metal doors of the car, begging that they stop and get out, all of them, and let Dad go. They should have taken me. I had admitted I was an accomplice in the building of the rocket ship. I was guilty of the crime of its concealment through these long summer months. I was the one who should be punished. Then the moment passed, and trembling with fear, I crept back into bed and clutched my pillow as if it were a life jacket holding me afloat on a wild storm-tossed sea.

A long, deadening silence followed, and it seemed to deepen, like the imaginary ocean I floated on. Then I heard Dad saying something as he came up the stairs. My body un-tensed, and my breath returned to my lungs: They had not taken him with them after all.

Still, I pretended to be asleep as he opened the door a crack to check on me, afraid I might otherwise break the spell that had brought him back to me and saved me from the Father Inquisitor, even if only for the moment.

I lay there a long time, heart pounding, unable to sleep.

As I lay there, a strange thing happened: my fervent relief transformed itself degree by degree into an intense glowing coal of anger.

Had Jim known what the consequences of his flight would be for those he had left behind? Had he ever once bothered to think about us? I was the one marked out for attention by the junta over the launch of the rocket ship. I was the one who had to return to school to face the commune louts Jim had been so quick to disassociate himself from. Dad had had to confront the Father Inquisitor to defend Jim and me, and in doing so, he could have been labeled a collaborator, perhaps even a saboteur. And it seemed to me there was still a terrible danger of that happening. Mom was caught in the middle of all this, beside herself with anguish.

Jim, on the other hand, had thought of no one but himself.

I climbed out of bed, pulled on my nightgown, opened the attic window, and scrambled onto the roof. I sat with my knees tucked under my chin and looked up at Little Sister. Its face was dark. The lights were turned off in all the houses up there, and everyone was asleep.

I was beginning to see Jim in a different light.

I had mistaken his selfishness for determination, his few words for wisdom, his aloofness for maturity, and his tolerance of my presence as kindness. I had been wrong on all counts. He had been nothing of the sort, merely obsessed, monomaniacal, introverted, and uncaring. The whole affair of the rocket ship had been about him, about *his* need to find *his* birth mother and his other family, and in doing so, he had turned his back on his real family, the one that nurtured him and loved him.

I thought hard, sitting there on the roof as the Sun's pre-ignition began to lighten the sky. I thought about how he was not my real brother at all. And I thought to myself: I am nothing like him after all, and he is nothing like me.

I no longer looked up at Little Sister for a sign.

Jim had taken himself out of my life.

I decided to take him out of mine.

I crept back into bed and slept through the rest of the day. Mom and Dad did not have the heart to wake me for school.

Over that weekend, I took everything Jim had ever given me, everything I had ever pilfered from his room, all his pictures, anything that reminded me of him, and stuffed it all into a large pillow cover. Then, I shoved the pillow cover all the way to the back of my closet and covered it under a pile of winter jackets.

I sat at my desk, staring at my homework, feeling cold and determined.

It wasn't over, though. Not yet.

THE FOLLOWING WEEK, back at school, there were new whisperings, more sideways looks and nudged elbows, more of the sly glances I had seen when Jim had made his crazy flight to Little Sister.

"Jimmy Landsdowne has been returned!" they whispered, "They have sent him back!"

"Or whatever is left of him," the older boys crooned with relish.

I sat in class feeling as if I were made of lead, hearing those words again and again, "…has been returned…has been returned…"

In my mind's eye, I saw Jim lying cold on the kitchen table, his body mangled, grey, and lifeless, all the blood drained from it.

At the end of the school day, I packed my bag and walked home, not wanting to take the omnibus or go back at all, afraid of what might be waiting for me. Mom was sitting at the table in the kitchen, looking strained and white-faced. I stopped in the doorway. She turned and smiled a brittle smile at me.

"Joshua."

"Mom." I came up to the table and looked along its length for evidence that Jim's body might have been lain there. There was no blood, no gore, nothing at all.

"They are saying, at school…" But I couldn't bring myself to repeat the whispers.

She nodded and turned away, closing her eyes. There were tear stains on her cheeks.

Dad found me in my bedroom, contemplating the bulging pillow cover.

"The militia has him," he said in response to my question. "I've seen him. But only at a distance. They wouldn't let me talk to him. He's…"

"I want to see him."

Dad looked at me, perplexed.

I gritted my teeth. "Dad, I helped him build that ship. I kept it a secret, so it was my fault Jim got himself and us into this whole mess. I want to see him. I have to go." I spoke with great intensity.

Dad pursed his lips, looking troubled. "I'm not sure it's a good idea, Joshua. He's not, not…"

"I don't care what's happened to him. I have to, Dad," I said, tears prickling my eyes.

We cycled along the track to the old highway and then east to the concrete fortress that housed the headquarters of the Supreme Council for National Unity. The main gate, set in the thick concrete outer wall, was made of steel bars. The guards made us walk up to the bars with our hands over our heads and then questioned Dad through them, submachine guns in their hands. We waited while one of them disappeared, the other guards watching us impassively.

After a while, I sat down on the dusty road, my legs tired. A guard told me to stand up. I stood. Dad offered to carry me, but I shook my head. It seemed like an age before the other guard returned with a militia officer. There was a lengthy discussion. Then, the officer pointed at me.

"Him, the boy, the brother, only. They can talk for a few minutes, that's all. Nothing more. After that…" the officer shook his head.

Dad protested. The officer shrugged, pointing at me again, repeating his instruction. Dad remonstrated. The officer turned away and started to walk back inside.

"I'll go!" I called out after him.

Dad looked at me, tense and unhappy.

"Joshua. I'm not sure it's a good idea to go there alone. I'm not sure it's…safe." He looked back at the steel-barred gate and the windowless concrete walls.

A guard opened a small barred wicket gate in the main gate. "Are you coming or not?" he demanded.

"Joshua…"

I squeezed Dad's hand, "Please! This might be the only chance we have to talk to him. Just wait here!"

"Be careful. Very careful." He managed a strained smile. "And tell Jimmy…tell him we love him."

The little wicket gate slammed shut with a clang behind me. I had one last glimpse of Dad before I was shoved into a small, bare room with four metal chairs lined up along one wall and told to wait. I waited a long time. But I could be patient when I wanted.

A guard came and ordered me to follow him. He marched me across a small courtyard, through a heavy iron door, and then down a flight of steps. I was struck by the smell—the same smell of the rotting saboteur corpse in the square.

The first guard handed me over to a second guard, who took me through another steel-barred gate. We stood in a long concrete corridor lined with metal cages. The scene struck me as bizarre, as if some curious agricultural installation had been misplaced underground. There were three tiers of wire mesh cages lining either wall. Long sloping gutters on either side passed under the cages to catch the filth that fell from them. But it wasn't animals that were locked inside them. It was men. Through the mesh of the nearest cage, I could see a naked man spattered with excrement and with matted, greasy hair and a knotted beard, clutching the wire mesh and staring vacantly at the cages opposite. In another cage, a naked man sat with one arm manacled to the cage and the other missing at the shoulder. And there…my heart lurched in my chest. A naked boy lay curled up against the rear of his cage, his back to me. I moved closer, desperate to see his face. The guard grabbed me by the shirt collar and yanked me away, then shoved me forward and pointed down the corridor. There were hundreds of men and boys here, all naked, all filthy, all bony and half-starved, lethargic with hunger. I looked away, focusing on the way ahead, steeling myself for worse to come.

Then we were through another door, and the stench of the cell block was closed off behind me.

I was taken down another flight of stairs into a series of rooms lit by red lights. Men in uniforms that I did not recognize were working at desks lined up in neat rows. I was taken to one of the desks. The man working there looked up at me. I took a step back in shock, unprepared for what I saw.

It was Jim. He looked at the guard who had brought me.

"I thought they weren't supposed to be let in?" He sounded irritated.

"Only the kid," the guard replied.

Jim turned to look at me. "Joshua," he said, his voice flat, devoid of emotion.

"You, you made it," I stammered. For all I had cooked my anger and resentment into a pungent stew, hot for the serving, I could not dish it out now that I saw him again. Instead, a visceral relief gripped me — Jim was alive and well.

He sat there, looking up from a blueprint he was working on.

"I thought…I was worried that…you know…"

Looking down at the desk, I was unsure what to say or do. He did not help me in my confusion.

At a loss, I asked, "What are you doing here?"

"Building a rocket."

Was he joking? I looked down at the blueprint again. It showed a drawing of a rocket broken into segments, with the metal skin peeled back to reveal all the complicated innards. This was a much more sophisticated rocket than the one we had built in the ravine.

"A rocket? What for?" I whispered.

"What do you think?" he said. A sly little smile curled the edge of his lips. "Do you know it was you who saved me?

They didn't believe I made that rocket until after the Father Inquisitor came and questioned you." But he didn't sound grateful, just proud. "After that, they brought me here and said I could work on the project that the Supreme Council says will free us once and for all from the tyranny of Little Sister. To design and build a bigger rocket and a bigger warhead. A rocket that is more reliable and much more accurate. So we can bomb them into submission."

"Why?" I asked. Some of the other workers looked up from their desks at me.

Jim's eyes narrowed, and he put his finger to his lips. Then he said, his voice low, "Why? *Why?* Because *they* want to break our world, break the will of the Supreme Council. Didn't you listen to the Father Inquisitor?" He pulled back his cuffs and showed me his wrists. Both were bandaged. He pulled back the edge of a bandage. I saw a thick black crust of blood and the stitching needed to hold the wounded flesh together. "They kept me trussed up like a pig from the moment I landed. Tied my hands to my feet, stripped me naked, dragged me over the stony ground, threw me in a cell. I almost bled to death from my injuries. And they wouldn't have cared if I had." He looked at his bandaged wrists. "If it hadn't been for the agreement between us and them, forced on them by those earlier missile attacks…"

"What about your, your…" Here was the line that could never be crossed. I forced myself to get the words out, "… your mother?" And I had crossed it.

"What?" He gave me a sharp look. "*What?*" He spoke as if I had uttered an obscenity.

But I had to know, so I asked again, "Your…real mother?"

His face contorted into a moment of ferocious anger, then became a stony mask of hate. "Her?" he hissed. "They keep no records of the mothers of boys. The birth of a boy is a curse and a humiliation for them. Boys are disowned and disavowed at birth. A woman there might kill a boy child if she thought she could get away with it."

I looked at the rocket and thought of Little Sister's cratered face.

As if sensing my thoughts, Jim said, "They hate us, Josh. All of us. They want every single one of us dead." He showed his teeth in an empty smile. "The Supreme Council for National Unity is right. They have to be bombed into submission. It's the only way our world can survive."

I whispered, "What about Mom? She loves you."

Jim hunched over the blueprint, staring down at it.

"She's not my mother."

Even though I had been expecting this response, the words were still like a knife in my heart.

I squeezed all the emotion out of my voice. "She brought us both up," I said.

"So? No one is going to bomb her. She's here already. *She* doesn't have to be forced back. But the rest have to be. So it's like it was before, again. Like it should be."

It was dark when they let me out. Dad was sitting with his back to the high concrete wall of the perimeter, sleeping fitfully. He woke up with a start as I walked up to him. "Joshua! Thank goodness! I thought, I thought...I don't know what I thought. I do know that I am so very pleased to have you back, though!" He gave me a bear hug, then, holding my shoulders, asked, "Jimmy, did you see him? Is he OK? Did you...talk to him?"

"Yes," I said.

"They are treating him well?"

"Yes."

"He is comfortable?"

"Yes."

"You're sure?"

Dad looked at me long and hard.

I nodded, "Yes, I'm sure, Dad."

"Did you give him our love?"

"Yes," I said, my eyes sliding away from his.

"And what did he say?" Dad couldn't hide the urgency in his voice. I had been sworn to complete secrecy. That was the price for seeing Joshua one last time. I could say nothing of what I had seen or passed between us.

So, I lied, one last time for Jim, to Dad, and later, to Mom.

END

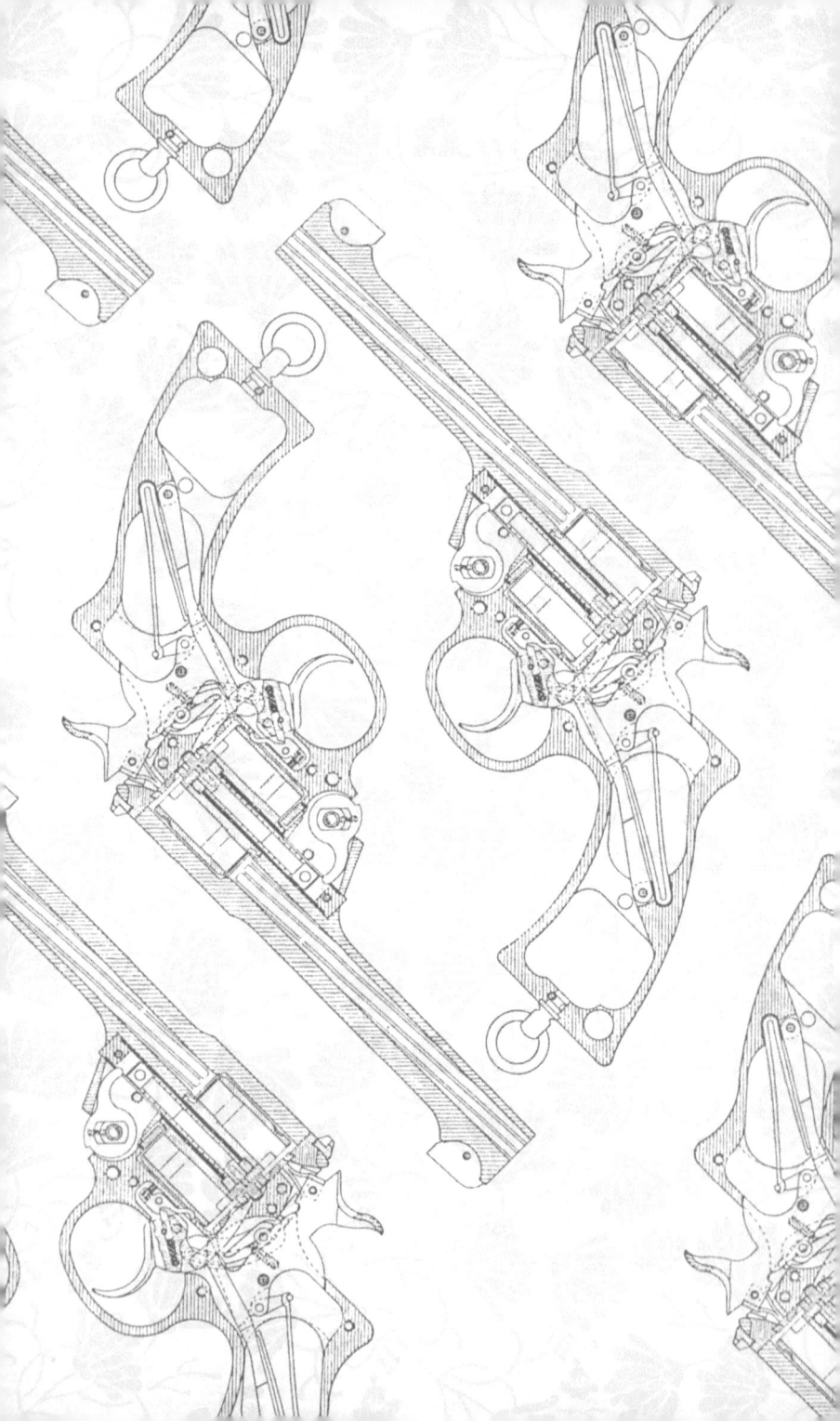

The Day It Snowed Forever

Part 1:
Mr Barnes

I SWEAR the first snowflake landed smack dab on Johnny Ray's nose. He stopped, looked at me wide-eyed, then looked up. I skidded to a halt on the bone-hard ice and looked up, too. The lumpy gray sky was full of snowflakes, floating down like fat, white butterflies that had forgotten how to fly. They tumbled about on the gusting wind before settling on the frozen ground, covering everything with a gentle white blanket.

"Geez!" Johnny Ray exclaimed, his eyes brimming with delight. "Snow. Just like Dad said. Here it comes!"

We slid about on the frozen creek, shouting and yelling, "Here I come!", "Banzai!" and "Look out!" with the powdery snow piling up all around us.

Johnny Ray crouched on the creek's bank, winding up for a big run-in. "Watch out!" he yelled and charged onto the creek. The moment his snow boots touched the ice, he slipped right over — *whump!* He was flat on his back and almost knocked me over as he came barreling past. I thought he was hurt, but no, running after him, I saw he was laughing fit to bust, and I started laughing fit to bust, too. I let myself fall onto my butt and went sliding up to where he was lying spread-eagled, tears of laughter running down his bright pink face.

"Let's do it again!" he panted, struggling onto his feet.

"Yeah, come on!" I shouted.

A howl — and I mean a *howl* — stopped us dead in our tracks.

We stared in the direction it had come from.

"What was that?" Johnny Ray asked in a small voice.

"I dunno."

The noise came again. This time, it was unmistakable: A wolf's howl.

Johnny Ray's eyes grew as big as saucers. "That's a wolf."

"Yeah," I said. "Reckon it is."

"Where's it coming from?" Johnny Ray asked, looking pale.

I pointed in the direction of the sound. "That way is the zoo."

"Yeah," Johnny Ray said. He watched the snow swirling about. "They can't get out of their pen, can they?"

"No." I shook my head and pulled my chin in. "No way. You been there a hundred times. You know that," I chided him.

"Yeah," Johnny Ray said uncertainly. He sniffed the air and pulled a face, like he was smelling wolf. "Maybe we should go home now."

"It's GOING to be a big storm," Mr Barnes said, leaning on his snow shovel. He was standing at the foot of the path leading up to his house. His house was next to ours, making him our neighbor on that side of the street. He was talking to Dad, who had been helping him clear his path. Dad was resting his snow shovel on his shoulder, holding it like a rifle, and saying something about a jet stream getting stuck.

I wanted to listen. What was a *jet stream?* And how could it get stuck? Johnny Ray and me were supposed to be distributing salt on the snow-covered sidewalk in front of our house. I was supposed to be distributing, and Johnny Ray was supposed to be directing. I got to throw the salt around, pretending to listen to Johnny Ray while he waved his arms about, pointing every which way like a madman. I mean, he was just a little kid, after all.

"Not so much on the garden or the grass," Dad advised, watching us for a moment before continuing his conversation about jet streams with Mr Barnes.

I edged closer to hear what they were saying. Mr Barnes was old. And I mean, really old. His hair was white, like snow, and wavy, and there was white stubble on his chin, and he had a stoop. He used his shovel like a walking stick when he wasn't shoveling. Regular as clockwork, I could see the dewdrop forming at the tip of his nose, like it always did when he was cold. And, boy, was it cold.

His wife, Mrs Barnes, died last year.

She died of cancer.

That's what Dad said. Cancer grows inside you like a disease.

Because Mrs Barnes lived next to us, and we knew her — she sometimes gave Johnny Ray and me candies, but she warned us we weren't allowed to tell Dad and, of course, I never did, but Johnny Ray couldn't keep his mouth shut — we got to go to her memorial service, in the Greek Orthodox Church, which wasn't the church we usually went to, but the one that Mr and Mrs Barnes went to. Because Mr and Mrs Barnes came from Greece, Dad said. Although you couldn't tell from the way they looked or spoke. Anyway, she was lying in a coffin near the altar and the cross with Jesus on it. We had to go and say goodbye to her, even though she was already dead. I didn't want to. It spooked me, even though I don't usually get spooked. But Dad said it was the polite thing to do. She looked like she was sleeping, lying in there dressed in her best clothes. She was perfectly still, and her skin was shiny like she had been polished. I wanted to ask Dad about that, but he put his finger to his lip and shushed me.

Mr Barnes cried when he went up to the coffin to say goodbye to her. I felt sorry for him and embarrassed, too, crying like that in front of everyone.

Johnny Ray jabbed me in the ribs. "Put more on the sidewalk!"

"Hey! Cut it out. The salt is my responsibility."

Dad had cleared the sidewalk only a little while ago, and it was already covered in a layer of new snow. I sprinkled more salt, watching the snow shrink away from the big crystals.

The job done, we tramped back to join Dad, who was still talking to Mr Barnes. Mr Barnes was saying something about an evacuation.

"We done the sidewalk, Dad!" Johnny Ray announced.

Dad smiled down at us. "Then salt around the truck."

"Yes, sir!" Johnny Ray said, giving Dad and Mr Barnes a smart salute. Mr Barnes laughed. Johnny Ray can be pretty funny sometimes, so I saluted, too.

Later, I asked Dad who was being evacuated.

"Oh, anyone who wants. I think it'll be mostly old people. Families with kids. Anyone having difficulty heating their house or getting hold of food. People will be housed in the school. Then the Army will move them to places where it isn't snowing."

"School? Which school? My school?"

Dad nodded. "Folks can more easily be looked after there.

You know, kept warm and fed while the Army brings in trucks to evacuate them."

I thought about the school being full of old people. "Is Mr Barnes going?"

Dad frowned. "No, Mr Barnes wants to stay in his house, even though I tried to persuade him to go."

"Why doesn't he want to go? Why does he want to stay?"

"To be close to all his memories of Mrs Barnes."

"Oh," I said, thinking of Mrs Barnes lying in the coffin in the Greek Orthodox Church, with her shiny skin. "We're gonna stay, right?"

"Yes. The evacuation isn't mandatory. Yet."

"Huh?"

"People don't have to go. Not if they don't want to."

"So, we can look after him, can't we?" I said to cheer Dad up.

Dad sighed, "He's very old. He shouldn't be alone in such weather. I worry about him. What if he gets sick? It'd be better if he went with the rest of the folks. But there's no forcing him, that's for sure. He's a stubborn old man."

I thought of him crying by the coffin with Mrs Barnes in it. "I kind of understand why he wants to stay."

Dad looked sad, staring out the window and thinking about Mr Barnes, too, I guess. Then he smiled. "Perhaps you and Johnny Ray can visit him and keep him company for a little bit each day. How about that?"

I pulled a face. When I said, "We can look after him," I didn't mean John Ray and me. I didn't like Mr Barnes' house. It smelled funny, like polish. Maybe the same kind of polish they'd used to polish Mrs Barnes. It was a weird smell and made me edgy. Worse, everything was neat. I felt like I had to stay in one spot to avoid knocking into anything and breaking it. The idea of taking Johnny Ray to Mr Barnes' house on my own made my hair want to stand on end. Johnny Ray was like a bull in a china shop, at least according to Mom. She was always yelling stuff like, "Why can't you watch what you're doing? You're a human tornado, d'you know that?" as he went tearing up the stairs to get as far away from the scene of the crime as possible.

Being a human tornado was what Johnny Ray did around anything valuable or important. I don't understand why Mom hadn't learned that.

To please Dad, I mumbled, "OK," hoping he'd forget.

Another thought bothered me. "What if the Army says Mr Barnes has to go to the school? Do we have to go, too?"

"Don't worry. We are perfectly fine here. There is plenty of fuel oil for the furnace, so we'll have heating. The solar panels on the roof will provide electricity. Extra diesel for the car in the garage. Lots of food, lots of water. So, your mother and I have no plans to join the evacuation."

I nodded, relieved.

Johnny Ray came piling into my bedroom early the next morning, trying to yank me out of bed. He kept repeating, "You gotta see this! You gotta see this!"

I gave in and rolled out of bed. Dressed in our pajamas, we pressed our noses against the bedroom window. It was still snowing outside, and the snow looked real deep.

"Come on!" he insisted, hauling on my arm as he headed onto the landing and then raced downstairs, leaving me to follow.

We bundled into our winter gear, all dried out on the radiators, and I helped him put his snow boots on. Boy, was the snow piled up high against the front door. Of course, we didn't know that until we opened it. There was a wall of snow on the other side, taller than Johnny Ray.

"Wow," Johnny Ray said, kicking it before I could stop him.

"*No,* Johnny Ray!"

The wall collapsed. Snow tumbled into the hallway, knocking Johnny Ray over and cascading everywhere.

"Now, look what you did!"

"Wow," Johnny Ray said, sitting in a pile of snow up to his chin, his eyes bright with excitement. "Cool!"

"I think we better get the snow shovel." The pile of snow was already melting into the carpet.

We pulled on our gloves and hats and peered outside.

The ground seemed to glow because the snow was brighter than the lumpy gray clouds, making the world look upside-down. I wanted to turn my head on its side to get things right. One thing was certain: all the digging and salting we had done yesterday was gone, buried deep under the new snow.

"Dad is going to be so mad," Johnny Ray said with relish.

Getting the snow shovel was easier said than done because it was outside, on the front porch, and the snow was deep — up to my chest — making it difficult for me to tramp around in it and impossible for Johnny Ray. I used my gloved hands and brute force, with Johnny Ray egging me on from the open front door. I got hold of the shovel and shoveled the snow pile in the hallway back outside. One thing is for sure, snow shovels aren't so great for shoveling on carpets.

Once I had that done, I started digging my way across the porch. Of course, Johnny Ray had to join in. I went in front because the snow was taller than he was, and I was worried it might bury him if it caved in on him, and I'd never find him again.

We worked our way to the porch steps, with me digging and Johnny Ray trampling down the loose snow. Every so often, he would complain, "Hey, watch out for me!" as I threw the snow out of the way behind me.

"Let's see if we can get to the sidewalk," I said, puffing out great clouds of steam as I worked away at the snow.

"Yeah," Johnny Ray agreed. "I can't see any which way from where I am."

We dug our way down to the bottom of the porch steps, huffing and puffing, our faces and noses bright pink from the cold and our fingers numb inside our soaking mittens.

"This is hard work," I said.

Johnny Ray paused his trampling. "Yeah."

From behind us, through the open front door (which we had forgotten to close), we heard Dad's exclamation, "Oh, my God!"

We looked back.

"What happened here?" Dad was standing in the doorway in his dressing gown, a cup of coffee in his hand, looking down at the sodden carpet streaked with dirt and grit from the snow shovel.

Johnny Ray puffed his chest and bellowed, "It wasn't our fault!"

I shushed him and called to Dad, "The snow fell in when we opened the door! I had to shovel to out!"

"I can see that!" he said. Then, looking at us, "Where do you two think you're going?"

"To the sidewalk," I announced, and Johnny Ray echoed, "We're going to the sidewalk, Dad!" adding, "And don't try and stop us!"

I jabbed him with the handle of the shovel. "Shush your mouth!"

Dad laughed and returned his attention to the carpet. "Goodness! What a mess. Wait until your mother sees it."

We watched him step gingerly onto the porch where Johnny Ray had tramped the snow into a lethal ice patch.

"Hey, don't mess up our path!" Johnny Ray yelled, protective of all the hard work we'd done.

"Don't you two go anywhere while I get dressed. I'm going to get the other snow shovel from the garage." He disappeared back into the house, forgetting to close the front door.

"See what you did," I hissed at Johnny Ray.

Johnny Ray screwed his face up into a grimace and tried to punch me in the arm. I pushed him, and he slipped over, falling flat on his back.

"Hey!" he complained.

"Just trample, and don't cause trouble," I warned him, and we returned to our expedition, me digging and Johnny Ray trampling.

WHEN DAD REAPPEARED, we had reached the sidewalk, creating a ragged trench cut through the snow.

"We did it! We did it, Dad!" Johnny Ray yelled, jumping up and down and slipping again on the treacherous ice path he had created. I hauled him back onto his feet.

"Well done! Now, come back here and get some hot breakfast inside you. I've got something to show you!"

"What? What?!" Johnny Ray called back, excited.

"Come and see!"

After warming up and finishing our snacks, Dad asked if we planned to go out again. I knew Dad was joking — it would have taken wild horses to stop us — and Johnny Ray bounced up and down in his seat, calling out, "Yes, yes!"

"Well, then. *I* knew the storm was coming and found these at Jempson's store. You'll need them to get around in all this snow." He tossed two pairs of ski goggles to us.

"These are just ski goggles," Johnny Ray complained.

"Ah, but I have something else." He held up two odd-looking pairs of plastic paddles, one pair smaller than the other.

"What are those?" Johnny Ray demanded, looking suspiciously at the paddles.

"Snowshoes," Dad explained.

"They look like paddles to me," Johnny Ray said, not mollified by Dad's explanation.

"You put them on your feet. See, these straps fit over your boots. Come on. Let's try them on and try them out."

THE CLOUDS HAD DISPERSED, turning the morning into a crystal-clear day in 8K right onto the surface of my eye.

The sky was a dizzying blue. When Johnny Ray leaned back and looked all the way up to the top, he toppled over into the snow, laughing. Everything else was a brilliant, blinding white, forcing us to strap on our goggles so we wouldn't go snow blind.

The snow had transformed the neighborhood into the surface of a strange, wintery planet. The road outside our house had disappeared, and the cars parked along the sidewalk had disappeared, too. In their places were hillocks of snow marking their graves. The only evidence of the sidewalk was the deep footprints where someone had struggled through the drifting snow.

Johnny Ray and I lumbered around on our bright plastic snowshoes, walking stiff-legged until we got used to them and how they allowed us to walk on top of the snow instead of through it. Well, most of the time, at least.

The street was empty, and most of the houses, buried halfway up their ground-floor windows, were dark. We clumped and puffed up the gentle incline to the top of the street. At the corner of the school playing field — a smooth, undulating plain of the purest, untouched white (our eyes widened, and our hearts quickened at the sight) — we came across a group of adults.

"Like penguins," Johnny Ray said under his breath, frowning. He was right. They looked like so many penguins in their jackets and coats, thick trousers, boots, gloves, woolly hats, and ear muffs.

We listened as they said, "More snow coming," and looked at the sky with grim faces and pink noses.

"Jet stream has looped out from the Arctic."

"All the down the Eastern Seaboard."

"The whole Eastern seaboard," they said, disbelieving.

"Even Florida."

Johnny Ray nudged me, "Where's Florida?"

I pointed, "That way," then shushed him. I wanted to listen.

Someone else, with a funny accent, was saying, "Here to stay."

"Going to be stuck. For weeks."

"How's that even possible?"

"Global warming."

"Bullshit. It's fucking freezing," the man with a funny accent said.

Johnny Ray and I looked at each other, our eyes wide.

A big grin spread across Johnny Ray's chops, and he put his finger to his lips. Those were words we could not say in the presence of adults, although we occasionally practiced using them on each other, and had to stifle our fits of laughter, in case we were overheard.

The man with the funny accent continued, "Their heads are up their jacksies. More like global cooling."

"Heating interferes with the polar vortex and makes the jet stream less stable."

"Nah, they're just making that stuff up."

"I heard someone say it's like this huge stationary wave in the atmosphere."

"Ah, come on!"

"No, it's true. It's like a wave train in a river below a dam outlet. Troughs and peaks. We're in a trough. Europe is also in a trough. They're getting pounded, too."

"Truth. I heard the skiing in Scotland is pure powder."

The man with a funny accent laughed like he didn't believe it.

"You won't be laughing when the glaciers start moving south," someone else said.

Johnny Ray pulled on my arm. "Come on. This is boring."

I hesitated. I wanted to know more about the jet stream loop. But there was the school playing field, with nary a footprint to besmirch it, just waiting for us.

The snow was so high that, with our snowshoes, we could just about step over the chain-link fence around the school playing field without getting snagged on the barbed wire. I say "just about" because (of course) Johnny Ray got caught on a loose piece of wire. It took an age to unhook him and left a long tear in the seat of his ski pants.

As we marched across the expanse of white, we marveled at its transformation from a place we knew into a place we didn't know at all.

Six big Army trucks were parked on the playground next to the school's Main Building. One had a snowplow attached to the front.

"Wow," Johnny Ray said. "Let's go lookit!"

"Not too close," I warned.

The trucks were camouflaged in green, so you could see them from a mile away. They had huge knobby tires and a big canvas-covered area behind the driver's cab. Benches were squeezed into the covered area. Three of the trucks had their engines running, making a satisfying *thudda-thudda-thudda-thudda* noise. We breathed in deep of the fragrant exhaust fumes.

"Wow," John Ray said again.

As we stood and watched, blowing clouds of steam into the icy air, people started emerging from the school and lining up by the trucks. Soldiers appeared with little stepladders to help the people climb into the trucks. Most of the evacuees had suitcases. The soldiers said, "No room for suitcases. Just leave them here."

"What about looters?" someone asked.

"Looters are gonna be shot on sight. So, don't you worry about no looters. All your belongings will be stored in the school. You can collect them when you come back."

One by one, the soldiers made a pile of discarded suitcases.

We saw kids from the neighborhood. There was Sally Ryans. Johnny Ray waved. I elbowed him. Then we saw Ilan Horowitz, George Sanders, Penny Taylor (I felt funny and uncomfortable as she walked by), and our neighbors from across the street, Jamie Whittaker and his brother, Alfie. Johnny Ray clumped to his feet and shouted to Alfie, jumping up and down on his snowshoes. Alfie looked around, trying to locate the source of the shouts. When he spotted us, he gave us a small, hesitant wave as if he was embarrassed to see us watching him with his family. Johnny Ray looked confused and disappointed and gave Alfie a small, unenthusiastic wave back. Jamie ignored me. I wasn't surprised. Him and me had had a spat over who had the best Lego Millennium Falcon. We had brought our models to school, and everyone had agreed his model was better. No one would listen to me when I told them Jamie's model was better only because it was the most expensive one in the store. I got mad and broke his model, smashing it with my fist. When he saw what I'd done, he started crying, like I'd thumped *him*. I felt terrible like I *had* thumped him. I didn't know what to do or how to say sorry, so I picked up my model and smashed it on the classroom floor. There was Lego everywhere. When Mrs Rhonda learned what had happened, I was sent to see the Head of School and put in detention for a whole week. Mom and Dad were livid when they learned what I'd done, and they made me apologize to Jamie in front of Alfie and his parents.

There was no way we could be friends after that.

The trucks were packed with people, squeezed onto the benches and the floor. They revved their engines, spewing thick black exhaust, and rumbled across the playground, one after another, falling in behind the truck with the snowplow, which scraped across the tarmac, making a gritty, grinding sound. John Ray grimaced and clamped his mittens over his ears until they were gone.

We examined the pile of discarded luggage in the playground.

"They're gonna get buried under the snow," Johnny Ray observed.

"They sure is. I wonder if they'll be able to find them again."

Johnny Ray frowned. "My butt's freezing."

"Well, if you'd been more careful climbing over the fence, you wouldn't have a hole the size of Nebraska in your ski pants."

Johnny Ray twisted around to look at the hole. "Mom's going to kill me," he said, looking pleased.

I could feel the cold seeping into my snow boots, and, like Johnny Ray, I wanted to get somewhere warm. People were milling around outside the school's main entrance, and we could see more people inside, through the windows, occupying our classrooms.

"Let's go have a look inside."

I took off my snowshoes and helped Johnny Ray with his so we could walk across the cleared playground past the remaining Army trucks. A soldier with a rifle stood guard at the school entrance and watched us as we approached.

I felt nervous under his gaze. "Can we go inside?"

"The school is for evacuees only."

Johnny Ray was having none of that. "My butt's freezing," he said, turning to show the soldier the gaping tear in his pants.

The soldier laughed. "Do your parents know you're here?"

I nodded, explaining we were walking around the neighborhood and wanted to get warm before we headed home again. He waved us through.

Inside, people were crowded everywhere: in the corridors, classrooms, and even the school gym. Some were sleeping on mats and inflatable mattresses or sitting around on school chairs or folding chairs. Our school desks were stacked in rickety piles along the walls to make more space. There were tall heaters, like lamp stands, everywhere, too. The place was toasty warm.

The gym was so crowded I was worried I'd lose Johnny Ray. I held him by the fur-lined hood of his snow jacket to ensure he didn't wander off. Soldiers were serving food under the folded-up basketball hoops: Soup and bread. The soup smelled good, and Johnny Ray asked me if he could have some. We shoved and pushed our way to the soup table, and I asked the lady soldier doling out the soup, and she said, *Yes, of course, darling*, and we got a bowl each and some bread. We sat in the hall with a bunch of other kids, several of whom we knew. They said they were going to be evacuated like it was a big deal. They had brought their favorite toys and games with them in their suitcases.

We didn't tell them about the pile of suitcases in the playground, slowly disappearing under the snow.

———

THE SNOWFALL GOT HEAVIER in the afternoon. Then the wind started to blow, swirling the snowflakes around so they twisted and spiraled about like crazy before piling up on the drifts that had already formed. I watched from the front window while the path we had dug to the sidewalk, which Dad had widened, gradually disappeared. The hump that marked our truck grew and then shrank as the snow piled up around it. The road disappeared, too, even though the Army snowplow had cleared it for the evacuation trucks.

Kneeling on the sofa, with my elbows on the windowsill, comfortable and cozy, I was mesmerized, watching the storm. It didn't seem like a storm, though. How could snow be a storm? Snow was strange and fantastical. It changed something boring into something magical, not like rain at all.

Later, when day turned to dusk, I wandered down to the Games Room in the basement. I played foosball with myself for a while, then explored the space behind the washing machine to see if there were any wild mice down there. (We'd had one living in the basement last year.) Then I rummaged through the junk in the toy box, looking for something to do. I could hear Dad, next door, working on the furnace. Bored, I joined him, squatting down to watch as he checked the dials, switches, and glass tubes.

"Are we gonna be warm enough?" I asked.

Dad nodded, considering the gauges. "Yes, we'll be fine."

The furnace made a *whoosh* and then a dull roar as the gas jets ignited. I could feel the heat from the flames and see their bright blue-white fingers through the grill. The heating pipes emerging from the top of the furnace started *tick-tick-ticking* as they heated up.

"Can we have a fire in the fireplace?"

Dad shook his head. "No, not today, with all that wind. We would lose too much heat through the chimney flue. And we should save the wood for later when we need it."

"How long will the storm last?"

"I don't know, Austin. The forecast says for another couple of weeks, at least. After that, who knows?"

I thought about that, then asked, "What's a jet stream?"

"Why do you ask?"

"I heard some people by the school saying we're stuck in it."

"Hmmm," Dad nodded, tightening a valve. "It's a wind that circles the North Pole. High up, and it's cold. Sometimes, part of it loops down from the Pole and comes way far south, bringing freezing weather with it, like now."

"How does that make us stuck?"

"Well, *we* aren't stuck. We can leave whenever we want. It's the jet stream that's stuck. Right over the top of us. And most of the way down the east coast. So, we are having weather like they have at the North Pole, where there are polar bears and it is always very cold."

"Will it be warm up there? What will the polar bears do?"

"Let's not worry about them right now. Just make sure we look after ourselves. And Mr Barnes. Will you go and see him tomorrow? And take Johnny Ray with you. That'll cheer the old man up. Mom has baked a chicken pie for him. If you give it to him, he won't be proud about refusing help from his neighbors, and we can be sure he'll be eating good, solid food and not get hungry or weak." Dad put his hand on my shoulder. "Can you do that for me, Austin?"

I didn't want to. Like I said, Mr Barnes' house smells strange and was too neat, an old person's house that wasn't meant for children. But I couldn't refuse Dad, even though I wanted to. The chore would be much less fuss If I left Johnny Ray behind.

I nodded and sighed. "Yes, I'll do it, Dad."

Dad smiled and hugged me. "Good boy."

JOHNNY RAY and I were playing foosball when Dad came in and shooed us out of the Games Room.

"Why?" Johnny Ray demanded.

"Because I have to do something private."

Johnny Ray crossed his arms over his chest. "Can't you do it somewhere else?"

"No. Now, out you go."

We trooped out, and Dad closed the Games Room door behind us. We sat on the sofa bed and listened to whatever Dad was doing. There was a rattle of metal-on-metal somewhere high up, the tinkle of a key ring, and the sound of the filing cabinet Dad kept in the Games Room being unlocked, then a sliding drawer being opened.

Mom came down the basement stairs with a basket of washing.

"You can't go into the Games Room because Dad's in there," Johnny Ray warned her.

"Well, really!" She raised an eyebrow at Johnny Ray. "We'll see about that."

We watched as she opened the door with a flourish, saying, "Ah ha!" as if to catch Dad doing something he shouldn't. Only, he was doing something much more interesting.

Seeing what was happening, Johnny Ray was up like a shot, yelling, "Dad's got a gun!" as he tore past Mom. And it was true; Dad was holding a gun in his hand. It looked like a real gun, too — a pistol, like a cowboy's six-shooter. Johnny Ray bounced up and down, tugging on Dad's trouser leg, begging, "Can I see it? Can I see it? Dad! Dad! Can I see it, Dad?"

Mom looked angry. "You know I hate having that thing in the house," she said as she edged past Johnny Ray and the foosball table to get to the washing machine. "I wish your father had never left it to you."

"It's a family heirloom!" Dad complained. "Might need it to hunt for food," he joked in a thick cowboy accent.

"Or shoot wolves?" Johnny Ray asked.

Dad looked puzzled. "Why would I want to do that?"

"We heard the wolves in the zoo howling when we were down by the creek."

"Johnny Ray is worried they might break free if the snow fills their enclosure," I explained.

"Oh, really? Well, yes. This is the perfect wolf gun," Dad said, drawing a bead on the door to the basement toilet.

Mum said, "I sincerely hope that thing is not loaded."

"It is not," Dad confirmed, popping out the cylinder and spinning it to show her the six empty chambers.

Mom was not satisfied with this demonstration. "Just make sure it is safely locked up, so no prying little thieves ever, ever get their hands on it." She tousled Johnny Ray's hair and gave me a significant look.

Dad nodded. He put his knuckle to his cheek and, sighting down his finger like he was sighting down the barrel of a gun, said, looking straight at me, "Austin, I want you to promise, with your hand on your heart, that you will never, ever open this cabinet and so much as peek at the gun, let alone lay a finger on it."

I nodded. "Yes, sir."

"Hand on heart," he commanded.

I put my hand on my heart.

"Now, say after me: I promise I will never, ever open this cabinet and touch the gun."

I did as he said.

"Very well," he concluded. "That's that. Yes?"

"Yes," I nodded.

"Now, I know you are curious, so I will let you look, but that is all."

Johnny Ray crowded around the weapon. I stood back, chastened by the seriousness of the promise I had been required to make.

"Can I see the bullets?" pleaded Johnny Ray.

Dad reached into the filing cabinet drawer and pulled out a box. He took a bullet out of the box and gave it to Johnny Ray. "Carefully, now. Don't drop it." He looked at me. "Do you want to look at one?"

I shook my head, even though I was desperate to take one. I watched Johnny Ray roll the bullet around in his cupped hands, a look of fierce concentration on his face. The brass case glinted, and the grey metal tip was pointed and mean-looking. There was a little circle on the base for the firing pin.

Dad was examining the gun, blowing dust out of the barrel, operating the trigger, and popping the cylinder in and out. Satisfied everything was OK, he asked Johnny Ray to return the bullet. Johnny Ray handed it back to Dad with exaggerated care. I sighed. Dad put the bullet back in the box.

"Are you going to shoot it?" Johnny Ray asked, excited. "Please, Dad, please!"

"Don't be silly, Johnny Ray. You never fire a gun inside a house."

I didn't say anything. I loved how the revolver looked; it was a proper cowboy's gun. The bullet, though — that made me shiver. There was something ruthless and indiscriminate about it: It would kill whoever or whatever it was shot at, even if it was someone you loved.

I WAS HOPING Dad would forget about asking me to go over and see Mr Barnes. And he might have, too, if it hadn't been for Mom's chicken pie. She had made it for Mr Barnes, and she wasn't going to let me forget.

"Austin, when are you going over to Mr Barnes?"

"Do I have to, Mom?"

"Yes, you do. You told your father you would. So, you will take this pie over for him and make sure he's alright."

"Can't you take it?" I pleaded.

"Austin, who do you think you are? Who makes all your meals for you, who washes your dirty dishes for you, who washes your clothes for you, who looks after you when you get sick? I do, and I don't ask for a penny in payment or even a kind word. Just the very smallest of favors, and you can't be bothered? What do you think would happen if I couldn't be bothered to cook your food? Or wash your dishes? Or…"

I put up my hands in surrender. "OK, OK, I'll go, Mom. Give me the pie."

She wrapped it in foil paper and then eased it into a shopping bag, warning me not to drop it. "And be sure to tell him he does not need to bring back the pie dish. You will come and collect it later once he has finished the pie. OK?"

"OK, Mom," I said, unable to hide the annoyance in my voice.

Honestly, why did I have to trudge over there? Just because no one else would? And in weather like this? What if I slipped and fell and broke my leg, and no one noticed? I could die out there. All because of a stupid pie. I wished the Army had made Mr Barnes evacuate with the rest of the neighborhood. At least Mom had forgotten (or didn't know) that Dad had asked me to take Johnny Ray, too.

Johnny Ray's eyes lit up when he saw me pulling on my cold-weather gear. "Hey! Where are you going?"

I grimaced. "To Mr Barnes' house."

"Oh," Johnny Ray said, examining a loose thread in his hoodie top. "You wanna play *Destructo Derby* when you get back?"

"No, not with you, that's for sure."

"OK," Johnny Ray said breezily and raced back upstairs, causing Mom to yell from the kitchen, "Will that herd of elephants please quiet down!"

The pie was so big and heavy in its dish inside the shopping bag that I had to carry it in both hands. It was big enough to feed a small army, let alone Mr Barnes. Mom opened the back door for me with yet another warning not to drop the pie. She didn't say anything about me slipping over and breaking my neck. At least Dad had cleared the snow in a path leading to Mr Barnes' back door. I put the pie in its bag on the step and rang the bell. Nothing happened. I rang the bell again and could hear the bell *bong-bong-bonging* inside the house. I stood for a minute and then rang the bell once more.

I was going to freeze to death before Mr Barnes came for the stupid pie. I gave the bell a long, hard press so there was no chance he'd fail to hear. The windowpane in the door revealed an empty kitchen. He had to be inside because, sure as heck, he wasn't going anywhere in this weather. Which meant I was going to have to find him. I, for certain, didn't want to lug the pie home. I'd only have to return with it later. Nor could I leave it on the step. Mom would have a hissy fit if I didn't deliver it into Mr Barnes' hands. I slogged through the new-fallen snow around to the front door. It took an age, so long that my feet went numb with cold. I rang the front door ball, a good long blast, so he'd know how irritated I was. I waited, the pie between my feet, beating myself across the chest with my arms to prevent frostbite and hypothermia from setting in. Still no Mr Barnes. I rang the bell, thumped on the door with my mitten fist, and shouted his name for good measure.

Maybe he'd gone deaf?

I clambered through the mountain of snow on Mr Barnes's porch to look through one of his front windows. I had to cup my mitten'd hands against the freezing glass to see inside. It was murky inside because the snow was piled up against the other ground-floor windows, and it took a few seconds for my eyes to adjust. When they did, I could see Mr Barnes lying on the floor. He looked like he'd fallen over. His face was turned away from me, so I couldn't see if he was awake or not. I forgot about the pie and galumphed back through the snow as fast as I could.

I was gasping when I got home and could hardly speak.

Mom looked concerned. "What is it?"

"Mom, Mom!" I wheezed, "Mr Barnes is lying on the floor!"

"What do you mean?"

"He won't answer the doorbell and is just lying on the floor!"

"Is he awake?"

"I couldn't tell."

Mom called up to the attic, "Dad! Dad! Come quick."

An irritated response came from far above: "What is it, Mother? I'm in the middle of dealing with the solar panels!"

"It's Mr Barnes, darling. He's fallen over and isn't getting up."

There was a brief silence. Then we heard the hurried *clomp-clomp-clomp* of Dad's feet on the stairs. He'd been up on the roof and was in his snow gear. "OK, where is he?"

"Austin saw him," Mom said, standing behind me with her hands on my shoulders.

Dad said, "What did you see?".

"He's lying on the floor downstairs. I could see him through the window."

"Was he awake?"

"I couldn't tell."

Dad was out the door and striding through the snow before I could blink. I hurried behind. When I caught up with him, he was banging on the window and calling Mr Barnes' name.

"He's alive. I can see him moving." Dad rattled the front door handle. "I'm not going to get in this way." He moved back to the window and tried to open it. "Gonna have to break it," he said with a sigh. He picked up Mr Barnes' shovel and used the handle to smash a pane of glass. It broke with a crash. Dad broke off the bits of glass sticking out from the frame and climbed inside. All the time, he called out to Mr Barnes. I didn't hear any response. I tried to follow, but Dad told me to wait where I was. He knelt by Mr Barnes and spoke softly, asking him if he was alright. Mom appeared at my shoulder, dressed in her cold weather gear, a bobble hat pulled down over her ears. She was holding the pie. I guess she picked up where I left it by the front door.

"Is he alright?" she asked Dad through the broken window.

Dad had his face close to Mr Barnes's head as if he were listening to something Mr Barnes was saying. He turned to Mom at the window, looking worried. "He's telling me it's congestive heart failure. We've got to get him to a hospital straight away."

"Can you get the front door open?"

Dad nodded. We heard him working the lock, and the front door swung open. Mom hurried inside, ignoring all the snow that tumbled in with her. I followed.

Mr Barnes lay slumped beside his sofa, his legs under the coffee table. His face and hands were white. It looked like there wasn't a drop of blood left in his frail old body. His lips were bright blue, and I could see he was mouthing something. Mom leaned close, listened, and then looked up at Dad. "He says there is medication in his bedside drawer."

Dad put his hand on my shoulder. "Can you go upstairs and find Mr Barnes' medication for him?"

I nodded.

"Good boy. Be quick, now." To Mom, he said, "I'll get the sled so we can move Mr Barnes to the truck."

"Dan, the roads. There's no way…" Mom said in an urgent voice.

"I've got to take him," Dad said. "He…he's very ill," then, to me, where I was, stock still, staring at the three of them — Dad standing, Mom kneeling, and Mr Barnes lying on the floor — "Off you go, Austin. Find that medication."

I clumped upstairs in my snow boots, leaving a trail of snow behind me. Mr Barnes's house was like our house. His bedroom was in the same place as Mom and Dad's bedroom.

I hesitated at the door, then walked inside. There was that same smell of polish, and I saw Mrs Barnes again, in my mind's eye, lying in her coffin with her eyes closed and her skin shiny as heck, like she'd been polished especially for the occasion. Everything in the room looked old. There were two narrow beds next to each other, unlike Mom and Dad's bedroom, which had one big, wide bed. One of the beds was neat and tidy. The other was unmade, the blankets and sheets all rucked and knotted. An old faded black-and-white photo was on the bedside table next to the unmade bed. The picture showed two young people, arm-in-arm, sitting on a low brick wall, smiling at each other. I could tell they liked each other from the expressions on their faces. They looked real happy together, there on the wall, the bright sunlight turning the background into an indistinct haze of nothing.

There was a whole load of junk in Mr Barnes's bedside table draw. More creased photos, used tissues, a random collection of coins, several ball-point pens, an old passport, a well-thumbed book of crossword puzzles, a whole bunch of paper clips, and three brown plastic medication bottles. Several types of pills were scattered among the coins and paper clips, but I ignored those, just taking the three bottles.

In the living room, Mom had moved Mr Barnes, so he was lying on his back with a cushion from the sofa under his head. His eyes were closed, and he was taking little panting breaths.

Dad came in through the front door with the big green plastic sled.

"Help me get him onto this."

Mom said to Mr Barnes, speaking close to his ear, "Fred, we are going to put you on our sled and move you to the truck so Daniel can drive you to the hospital."

I saw Mr Barnes shake his head, ever so slightly, from side to side.

Mom looked up at Dad, a pained expression on her face.

Dad shook his head emphatically: "There's no choice. We have to get him to hospital." Then he saw me. "Is that the medication?"

I held out the three plastic bottles.

"Here, give them to me," Mom said. She looked at the labels. "This one is an ACE inhibitor. This is a diuretic. And this one is some kind of digitoxin derivative. Mr Barnes, which one do you need to take? Mr Barnes?"

Mr Barnes did not respond, move, or open his eyes; he just kept breathing in shallow pants.

Mom made an exasperated noise. "Oh, Daniel! What the hell are we supposed to do?"

Dad was organizing the sled next to Mr Barnes. "The digitoxin? What does the dosage say?"

Mom examined the bottle. "One a day. Mr Barnes, have you taken your Digitoxin pill today? Is that the one you want?"

Mr Barnes made no response.

"Give him one pill. At this point, there is nothing to lose."

Mom leaned close to Mr Barnes. "Mr Barnes, I am going to give you a digitoxin pill. OK?" She took one from the bottle, eased it between his lips, and tried to push it between his teeth. The pill stuck in the side of his cheek. It was visible as a little lump.

"How is he going to swallow it?" Mom complained. "He needs something to drink. Austin, can you get a glass of water from the kitchen?"

I hurried to the kitchen. I found a set of china teacups and filled one from the tap. Walking back to the living room, I made sure not to spill any water on the snow-covered floor. Mom took the cup and tried to make Mr Barnes swallow the pill. Most of the water went down his chin.

"Aiy!" Mom made a frustrated noise.

"Look, let's get him into the car, then we can worry about

the medication. Austin, hold the sled while Mom and I lift Mr Barnes onto it."

Mr Barnes made a faint groaning noise as Dad, holding him under the armpits, and Mom, gripping his ankles, slid him across and onto the plastic sled.

"OK, Austin, here is the fob for the truck. Fold the seats down in back so we can lay Mr Barnes in there. Please?"

I nodded and ran outside, along the path Mom and Dad had trodden through the chest-high snowdrifts, and then the faint tracks left by the second convoy of Army trucks, to the mound marking the place where the truck was parked. I had to dig with my mitten'd hands to get to the driver's side door and then clear the snow piled up against the door, so I could open it, flinging the snow behind me. Johnny Ray appeared, his head poking into the space I had dug out of the drift. "Hey, can I help?"

"Sure. Get the snow out of the way."

He started shoving snow with great energy, matching my frantic efforts.

I opened the door wide enough to squeeze through the gap. Johnny Ray followed close behind. It was gray and shadowy inside the truck, with all the windows, except the driver's door window, buried in snow. The sounds were muffled like we were inside a world of cotton wool.

"What are we doing in here?" Johnny Ray asked, his eyes bright with excitement.

"Getting the back seats folded down so Mr Barnes can lie in the trunk."

"Why does he want to do that?" Johnny Ray asked, frowning.

"Pull on the handle, there, while I shove."

Johnny Ray did so, and with a heave, I folded the first of the rear seats.

"Now, the other one."

"Hey! Don't try and fold me up in it this time," Johnny Ray complained.

With both seats flat, there was a big expanse in the back of the truck. Johnny Ray bounced up and down on his knees. "Now, what?"

Snow fell away from the rear window, and Dad was there, wielding Mr Barnes's snow shovel. Mom was helping, too, and I could see the sled with Mr Barnes lying on it, bundled up in a bulging cocoon of blankets.

Dad had the tailgate door open in a minute or two, sending swirls of snow inside the truck. He handed me a pile of blankets. "Lay these out so we can lay Mr Barnes on them."

Johnny Ray and I organized the blankets while Mom and Dad maneuvered the sled up close to the back of the truck. With a "Hi-hup!" they hoisted Mr Barnes into the trunk, with Dad climbing in beside him and hauling him further in so he lay at an angle across the back with his head up against the front passenger seat. Johnny Ray, peering over the driver's seat at Mr Barnes's white face and open mouth, asked, "Is he dead?"

"No," Dad said curtly.

"Here's a flask of hot tea," Mom said, handing the flask to me, where I sat next to Mr Barnes in the back. "Try and get him to drink some."

I looked at the flask and Mr Barnes, where he lay on his side, his eyes half open. I winced. "I'm not sure, Mom."

She patted my shoulder. "Try."

"Now, Johnny-Ray, you will stay with Mom while Austin and I take Mr Barnes to the hospital. Can I rely on you to look after Mom?"

"Can't I come?" Johnny Ray asked, looking forlorn.

Dad repeated, "Can I rely on you to look after Mom?"

Johnny Ray folded his arms across his chest and pouted. "Why does Austin get to do all the cool stuff?"

"Because, Johnny Ray, I need you to do something much more important: Look after Mom."

Johnny Ray heaved a sigh. "OK. But next time, I get to go, right?"

"Next time, yes."

Mom put her arms out to pick up Johnny Ray. "Come on. Out of the car. Now."

Dad already had the engine running.

Mom said, "Have you got the extra diesel? Just in case."

"Yes, I have. It's on the roof."

She looked worried. "Take care. I love you both."

I always got nervous when Mom said, *I love you both*, like she thought she might never see us again. Dad leaned over and kissed her, and they smooched for a moment. I looked out of the window, irritated Dad hadn't left already.

"How is Mr Barnes doing?" Dad asked over his shoulder.

I shrugged, "He's the same."

Dad was distracted by the sudden slewing of the car on the icy road, making me spill scalding hot tea onto Mr Barnes' head. He didn't react. Dad wrestled the car back into the nearly invisible tracks the Army trucks had left behind. He hunched over the wheel, staring with concentration out of the windscreen. The snow had started again. Big flakes appeared out of nowhere, swirling around like they didn't know which way was down. They made little slapping noises against the windows as we ran through them. The only other sounds were of the engine revving when the wheels lost grip and Dad swearing under his breath every time they did. No one else was on the road, although seeing very far in any direction was impossible.

I glanced at Mr Barnes. I didn't like how he was staring at

the roof of the truck. So, I closed his eyes for him. He looked better with his eyes closed.

I poured another cup of the tea from the flask Mom had prepared, blew on it until it was cool enough to drink, and drank it down, so she wouldn't get angry that I hadn't managed to give any to Mr Barnes. I had tried, but it spilled down the side of his face. The tea tasted funny and smelled funny as if Mom had put sugar and some of Dad's bourbon in it. I pulled a face, but it wasn't so bad that I couldn't drink some more.

I watched the road ahead from my position in the back next to Mr Barnes. Everything was white: the sky, the ground, even the air. I couldn't see how Dad was able to drive at all. A big truck stuck in a snowdrift emerged out of nowhere, almost causing Dad to lose control. He swerved out of the way and we spun right around, coming to a stop facing the wrong way.

"Phew!" Dad said, looking at me. "That was close." He peered at the truck in the snowdrift. "That looks like one of the Army vehicles. Maybe someone can help us." But when we got out, we found the Army truck had been abandoned.

Dad whistled. "At least the hospital isn't much further."

We found the driveway to the main entrance was barred when we arrived. Dad had to get out and lift the barrier out of the way. We drove up to the entrance, stopping by a set of glass sliding doors. I couldn't see any lights on anywhere inside.

"I don't think there's anyone in there," I said. "It looks kinda dubious."

"Don't worry," Dad said. "Wait here, and I'll get someone to help us with Mr Barnes."

He jumped out of the car, leaving the engine running, and disappeared through the big glass doors. I climbed into the front passenger seat and put my gloved hands over one of the heater vents to dry my mittens. They were soaked with bourbon-smelling tea. I felt a little bit sick — from the tea, I guess.

Dad reappeared with another man. He was remonstrating with the man as he opened the rear door to the truck. An icy blast of air and a barrelful of snow swirled around Mr Barnes and me.

"Here he is," Dad said to the man.

The man was bundled up in camouflage gear and had a pump-action shotgun slung over his shoulder. Even so, I could tell straight away he wasn't a real soldier. He didn't have a cap or a beret, and there was no insignia on his jacket, and his trousers didn't match his jacket, and his boots were wrong. He was what Dad called a "weekend warrior" whenever we saw similarly dressed men out in the woods around our neighborhood. I didn't like how he ignored Mr Barnes and looked at Dad, the truck, and the jerry can of diesel on the roof.

Dad continued, "He needs immediate medical attention."

The weekend warrior was scanning the snowy expanse of the hospital parking lot and the tracks we had made as if he were checking to see if anyone else was with us.

"You got food?"

"No." Dad looked puzzled and annoyed. "No, we haven't. Our neighbor…"

"That's a can of gas up there," the man nodded at the roof rack. "We need gas."

"It's not gas, it's diesel. This old man…"

The weekend warrior unslung the shotgun from his shoulder and held it casually under his arm. "Look, buddy. There's a whole bunch of people sheltering in there," he nodded toward the hospital entrance. "Our need is greater than yours. You got more than enough. Get the gas can down."

"I don't know who you are, but he," indicating Mr Barnes, "needs help…"

The man turned so that the shotgun was pointing at Dad's feet.

Dad made a placating gesture. "OK, OK. I'll get it down. But only if you'll help me with this old man. He's in a critical condition."

"Sure. Get the gas down."

"Diesel," Dad corrected him again.

"Get it down, now."

Dad shook his head, exasperated. He clambered up on the rear wheel, unstrapped the diesel can, and heaved it down to the weekend warrior, who took it and lugged it over to the entrance. When he returned to the car, he said, "'Fraid there ain't no doctors left here no more. They all gone."

"This is a hospital. We have to get him inside," Dad insisted as if he hadn't heard what the weekend warrior was saying. "Please, could you just give me a hand?"

The man gripped the shotgun a little more firmly. "Look, buddy. I'm telling you, there's no doctors nor no nurses in there. That man ain't going to get no help here. So, there ain't no point."

"But, I saw them…"

"You didn't see nothing," the man said, his ugly face becoming hard and mean. Then, seeing me for the first time, his expression softened.

"That your boy?"

"Yes, he's been looking after Mr Barnes while I drove him here."

"He looks like a good kid."

Dad, perplexed and annoyed, said, "Yeah, he's a good kid. Takes good care of his little brother. Now…"

The weekend warrior interrupted, "I got a little brother. They always trouble, ain't they?" He addressed this question to me, a smile like a leer on his face. I nodded, not daring to speak.

To Dad, he said, "Just you don't go back in there, and there won't be no trouble for no one."

"Then how are we supposed to help this old man?" Dad said.

Pleading, I said, "Dad! Please, let's go!"

The weekend warrior looked from Dad to me and then to Mr Barnes. Perhaps he mistook the panic in my voice for concern about Mr Barnes because he seemed to relent and leaned into the car, taking Mr Barnes's hand from under the blankets. "I ain't no expert or nothing, but he sure don't look good. Looks like…" He laughed. "That old man, he ain't got no pulse. He's as cold as a catfish. He ain't alive, buddy. You wasted your time and your gas coming all the way out here with a dead body in the back of your truck. That's funny. That's real funny." His cold eyes were fixed on me. "Now, you get out of here. And you take that old man with you. We don't want his kind. And if you take my advice, watch out on the roads. 'Specially, seeing as how you got your boy with you. I wouldn't want no harm to come to a chil'. It ain't safe out there no more. It ain't safe nowhere."

I sat in the front with Dad on the way back home. We concentrated on the road. Dad drove more slowly now that there was no need to break our necks. Still, I wished he could have driven faster.

The pressure of Mr Barnes lying there, dead, drove a question out of me:

"Why are we bringing him back, Dad? Couldn't we leave him by the side of the road?"

I was shocked to hear myself say that. What was I? Crazy? Then I understood: I didn't want Mom to know I had let Mr Barnes die. She would find that pill still stuck in his mouth. If only I had tried harder to make him drink some of the tea, maybe the pill would have gone down, and maybe the medication would have saved him like she had hoped it would. Only, the car had been bumping all over the place, and I couldn't lift his head and try to make him drink at the same time. I felt tears of anger and self-pity come into my eyes, and I wiped them away before Dad could see.

Dad was peering through the windshield, looking tight-lipped and grim. He didn't reply or even turn to look at me. I wondered if it was because of Mr Barnes dying. Or because of what he had seen in the hospital. Or because we were lucky to have gotten away from that place in one piece.

After a while, I guess he forgot about what I had asked. Or maybe he didn't hear my question. I looked out of the window and had no idea where we were. Everywhere looked the same under the snow. Maybe we were lost and would keep on driving forever.

Then, out of nowhere, he said, "I am sure Mr Barnes would prefer it if he were to lie in rest in his own home."

I didn't say anything; I just thought of the picture by the bed, of the two young people sitting on the brick wall in the sun, smiling at each other.

Later, I asked, "Who was in the hospital?"

Dad sighed and shook his head. "There was no one in there."

I knew he was lying.

We dragged the body back to Mr Barnes' house on the sled. The front door was still open, and the big snowflakes had piled up inside, spreading into the living room and settling on the sofa, the armchair, and the coffee table where we had first found him.

I said, "Can we put him on his bed in the bedroom?"

"I thought you wanted to leave him by the side of the road?" Dad snapped at me, and I knew, from the pent-up frustration in his voice and the anger on his face that he was feeling the same as I had felt in the car coming back from the hospital.

"He would like that. He'll be closer to Mrs Barnes up there," I said, thinking of the photo and maybe Heaven, too.

Dad took a deep breath and let it out, shaking his head like the whole long day had been too much for him. And then he smiled, looking at me.

"I think you might be right, young man," and I smiled too — I liked it when he called me *young man*: It made me feel grown-up — "I think Mr Barnes would like that," and we both looked at him, where he lay, dead, on the plastic sled, in the hallway. "It'll be nice and cozy for him up there. Yes. Let's take him upstairs. Give me a hand?"

I nodded, and Dad struggled with him up the stairs, holding him under his armpits and stopping every five steps to catch his breath. Meanwhile, I gripped the cuffs of Mr Barnes's trousers, exposing his white hairy shins and the purple veins under his wrinkly, papery skin.

Dad put him in the unmade bed, laying him on his side so his closed eyes could face the photo on the bedside table.

"I think that's nice, don't you?"

It was freezing in the bedroom, and Dad's breath formed clouds in the air.

I said, "I think that's how he would like it."

When we left, Dad tried to close the front door but couldn't because the snow we had tramped in the entrance hall had turned to ice, preventing him from swinging it shut.

"I'll come back and sort this out later," he said.

But he never did.

"What did you see?" Mom asked.

I was sleeping with Johnny Ray on the fold-out sofa bed in the basement. We had moved down from the second floor to avoid heating the whole house, just the basement and the kitchen. The furnace was down here, which would help us stay warm and conserve heating oil.

Mom and Dad set up a bed in the Games Room (where the foosball table had been), and even though the door was closed, and I was supposed to be asleep, if I listened carefully, I could just about hear what they were saying.

"I don't know," Dad said. "I thought they were doing some kind of operation."

Mom sounded skeptical. "In a corridor? With no lights? And you didn't say anything?"

"I was worried about Mr Barnes. I was focused on him. Not what was going on in there. The place was in chaos. They were burning furniture. To stay warm. I guess that's why the man took the can of diesel."

"You just let him take it? When we might need it?"

"He had a gun, darling."

"Well, what about your father's gun? I never understood why you kept the damn thing. Then, right when you need it most, you didn't even think to take it with you."

"I could never have guessed what I would find at the hospital."

"Was Mr Barnes still alive, then?"

"I don't know. I don't think so. But I didn't know that, then. It took so long to get there."

"Why?"

"Why do you think?" Dad said, annoyed.

There was a *shushing* sound and a long pause.

Dad continued, his voice softer, quieter, calmer. "It was only afterward, after we left…The man in the combat gear, I thought he was, I don't know, in charge, a soldier, maybe, although it was apparent soon enough that he wasn't. But I didn't care at that point. I just wanted to get Mr Barnes to a doctor. The man said there were no more doctors. But I had seen what I thought was an operation in one of the corridors inside the hospital, so I insisted we needed to go and get Mr Barnes. At least, they had the means to help him even if there were no doctors."

"And?" Mom prompted.

"He took one look at Mr Barnes and saw that he was dead. I hadn't looked. I thought…"

I could feel the knot of anxiety tighten in my stomach. Dad was going to tell Mom about how I had let Mr Barnes die.

"He told us to leave and take Mr Barnes with us. And then I got it. It clicked. There was no hospital there anymore. No doctors, no nurses. And," he laughed, a kind of awkward, strangled laugh, "I think they might have been cutting up the person in the corridor."

"They were cutting him up?"

"Her. It was a woman. They were cutting her up. Like…" Dad's voice broke. "It was…"

I could hear him crying. My anxiety turned to shock. Dad, crying? I thought of the weekend warrior with the shot-gun. There had been something about his face, his eyes. I had known right away he was a wicked man, an evil man. My breath started coming more quickly, thinking about how close Dad had come to being shot.

There was another long pause.

Then Mom said softly, "If there's no hospital anymore, what if one of the boys gets sick? Or me? Or you?"

Dad said nothing for a while. "We have the medical supplies."

"I mean, really sick," Mom insisted.

"I'll drive."

"Through this snow?" Mom sounded skeptical.

Dad was unperturbed. "We'll need to get more diesel."

"There must be a dozen cars on the street."

Dad sighed. "All the cars around here are electric. No use. And those who could took off in their four-by-fours."

Mom said, "The snow extends hundreds of miles in every direction away from us."

"Maybe I can find a snow plow truck. I've seen one on 32nd Street before. Maybe…"

"Daniel, we can leave if needed, couldn't we?"

Dad was silent for a long time. "I can search, see what I can find, that truck with a snow plow shovel, and diesel. I'm sure it's possible."

It was Mom's turn to be quiet. Then, she said, "You have the satellite emergency call system. You can use that."

"But we aren't in an emergency. That's for life-and-death situations."

"How can this not be an emergency?" Mom insisted.

"It is, but not for us. I guarantee other people are in a much worse predicament than us. You know what it'll be like. There'll be refugee camps and all kinds of chaos. It might not be better out there. We might be better here."

"The Army will be in charge. There'll be medical help."

"Over a hundred million people live on the Eastern Seaboard. Where are they going to evaluate a hundred million people? And if the snow keeps on…the forecast says there is no end to this stall in the jet stream."

"It can't last forever." Mom said, disbelieving.

Dad didn't reply, and the silence stretched on until I must have fallen asleep.

Part 2:
The Weekend Warrior

SOMEONE WAS MOVING AROUND UPSTAIRS.

I lay in bed, listening. Johnny Ray was fast asleep next to me.

Whoever it was was treading quietly, like they didn't want to be heard.

For an instant, I imagined the man at the hospital, in camouflage gear, with the shotgun under his arm, walking around in our living room.

I sat up, mouth dry, my heart thumping.

There was a clunk, followed by a low curse, and I could relax.

It was just Dad using his favorite bad word — the "F" word.

I pulled on my clothes and padded upstairs. It was dark and cold in the living room and dining room, with all the windows made blind by the depth of snow piled against them. It felt like the middle of the night, but I could see from the clock on the microwave oven that it wasn't.

Dad must have gone upstairs to the second floor. I climbed the stairs and found him in Johnny Ray's bedroom, with the window looking out of the front of the house wide open. He jumped when he saw me.

"Aiy, Austin! You gave me a scare. I didn't hear you coming up behind me."

I said, "I thought you were that man from the hospital."

Dad smiled. "Well, it was brave of you to come up and investigate but, in future, always find me or Mom first if you think something odd is going on, yes?"

I shrugged. "OK." And then added, "But I knew it was you because I heard you swearing."

"Ah, right," Dad said, looking embarrassed.

"What are you doing?" I could see he was preparing to go outside.

"Well, I, umm," he frowned. "I was just going out to look around the neighborhood."

I noticed a bulge in his jacket pocket and saw the muzzle of the revolver poking out.

"Hey, Dad, is that the gun?"

"This?" Dad made a face, shoving the gun deeper into the pocket so the barrel was hidden from view. "Yes, it is."

I licked my lips. "Can I have a look?

He considered, a pensive expression on his face. "I shouldn't. Your mother would be livid with me if she discovered I'd been encouraging your interest in guns."

"I promise I won't tell her," I said, desperate to see the gun again. I held my breath.

"Well, alright," he said, giving in. He took the gun from his pocket and held it up for me. Now that I could look at it more closely, I saw the revolver was made of gray metal with a black grip. It had a long barrel with "Smith & Wesson" stamped into the metal. There was a sight on the front, over the muzzle, and the cylinder where the bullets went had these repeated indentations. Behind the cylinder was the rear sight and, behind that, the hammer sticking out of the body of the gun.

"What's that?" I asked, pointing at a little sliding button behind the cylinder.

"That? That's the cylinder release. It works like this." He pushed it down and forward, and out popped the cylinder. All the bullet chambers were empty.

"Where are the bullets?" I asked, disappointed that the gun was not loaded.

"In my other pocket," Dad said, patting his jacket,

"Where they are going to stay," he added, seeing my eyes light up.

I could feel my heart racing again, but from excitement, this time. "Can I hold the gun?"

Dad studied me for a moment. "Yes. But you must not tell Mum." He slid the cylinder back into the body and handed the pistol to me.

I held the grip in my right hand and the barrel in my left. The revolver was heavy, heavier than I had imagined it would be. "Can I open it?" Dad nodded and watched me press and push the little button above the grip. I eased the cylinder out, like Dad had, and almost dropped the gun. Dad said, "Be careful. It's valuable. Here, let me put the cylinder back for you." He took the gun, slid the cylinder back into the body, and returned it to me. I aimed it around the room and then aligned the sights on Dad.

"No, Austin! Never point a gun at someone, even if it isn't loaded."

I dropped the barrel, feeling my face redden. "I'm sorry," I mumbled.

"It's not your fault. I should have warned you." Dad took the gun off me gently. "Look, I am going to test it. Want to come along?"

I perked up, "Sure, Dad."

"OK. Get your boots and jacket and snowshoes, and we can go."

Once I was ready, we climbed out of Johnny Ray's bedroom window.

"Be careful on the snow," Dad said as he helped me strap on my snowshoes. "It's deep enough that you could disappear altogether!"

We trekked among the neighboring roofs, all that remained of the surrounding houses, until Dad found a place far enough away that the noise of the gun would not disturb Mom or Johnny Ray. He loaded the revolver with three bullets and shot at the top of a tree, poking out of the snow, *crack, crack, crack*, sending flurries of ice crystals into the air. I could see smoke and sparks shooting out of the muzzle and from between the cylinder and the body of the gun. The smoke was sharp in my nostrils, a kind of sulfury, burning smell I breathed deep into my lungs. Dad's face was red and flushed when he had finished, and his eyes bright with excitement.

He slid open the cylinder and used the extractor rod to push the spent cartridge cases out into the palm of his hand.

I crowded up close to see what he was doing.

"Can I have a cartridge case?" I begged.

Dad laughed, "No. I'm sorry, Austin. If Mom caught you with one, you and I would be for the high jump." He threw the three cartridges into the treetop, where they bounced off the branches and disappeared into the underlying drifts of snow. I stared hard at the spot, trying to memorize it.

"OK. The fun's over. Let's get back home for some breakfast. I'm starving! How about you?"

I nodded, "Yeah, me too."

THE SNOW CONTINUED FOR DAYS.

Or maybe it was weeks.

I couldn't tell.

We lost track of time, Johnny Ray and me. Every day was the same as the day before. Mom set us schoolwork to do, but it was impossible to concentrate on the lessons. We were distracted by the strange weather, by the loop of the jet stream trapped over where we lived. When the internet quit, Dad listened to the radio for news instead. Sometimes, I listened to the emergency announcements with him, but I found them boring. The bulletins detailed which refugee camps were accepting refugees, which roads were open, and where to get picked up by the Army if you needed to be evacuated. The weird thing was the western US was suffering the worst drought ever, with high temperatures never before experienced all across the region. There were water rationing and heat advisories, people dying of heat stroke, and wildfires burning towns to ash while we were perishing cold under a mountain of snow. When we looked outside, there was less and less to see. Just snow piling higher and higher and higher. The parked cars had long ago disappeared, and the street was only a slight dip in the drifts between our house and the Lawrences' house across the way.

Luckily, the first window to collapse was in the Lawrences' house.

Dad and I were outside investigating some paw prints.

"What do you think?" Dad asked. "Wolf?"

I stared at the big prints. They sure looked like wolf. "Where could they come from, though?"

Dad said, "The zoo?"

There was a muffled crash behind us. We turned. A hole gaped in a snowdrift by the Lawrences' house. We snowshoed over it.

"Window's caved in," Dad said, peering down the hole. "Under the weight of the snow." He looked back at our house. "We are going to have to board up our windows to make sure this doesn't happen to us."

We squatted on our haunches and stared down into the dimness.

I could just about make out the pile of snow that had spilled through the shattered ground-floor window.

"I wonder where the Lawrences are," Dad mused, rubbing his chin.

I thought about Jamie and Alfie leaving on the big Army truck. Had they been on the truck abandoned near the hospital? I hoped not.

"I'm going to take a quick look. Just to make sure everything is OK. You wait here. I don't want you getting cut on any of the glass down there."

Dad slid down into the hole and climbed through the pushed-in window. I could see his vague outline standing by a toppled chair. Then he disappeared from sight. I could hear him walking around on the broken glass. Then there was silence. I leaned down into the hole and called, "Dad? Dad!" Was he alright? Should I climb down and check? I thought about returning home and telling Mom, but I knew she'd be mad at Dad for leaving me alone, so I called again, "Dad! Dad!"

I almost jumped out of my snowshoes at a creaking sound behind me. For a moment, I thought it was the wolf who'd left the paw prints in the snow.

But it wasn't. It was Dad hauling open one of the bedroom windows on the second floor of the Lawrence's house. He gestured to me. "Come on. Come and see."

I took my snowshoes off and climbed through the window. We were standing in Jamie's bedroom. I could tell because there was the rebuilt model of the Millennium Falcon, the one I had smashed to pieces with my fists. It was eerie being in his room without him knowing. I followed Dad downstairs. Gray light filtered in from outside through the caved-in window. I could see the pile of snow that had cascaded into the dining room.

"The other windows are going to break at some point," Dad said. "We should take what we can before they do."

I looked at him. Were we going to steal from the Lawrences? I felt a little thrill of fear and excitement.

We searched through the kitchen cupboards, stacking cans on the counter. Dad opened the fridge and closed it with a bang as the powerful smell of rotting fish wafted around us.

"Aiy! That stinks!" Dad batted at the air before his face, and I covered my nose with a mitten. "The fridge ended up keeping the warmth in and the cold out. What a pity. Can you look around for some shopping bags?"

I found a whole bunch in a drawer, and we started filling them with cans and packets of dried food.

"Are the Lawrences going to come back?"

Dad paused, "I don't know, Austin. I hope so. Eventually."

"But if they do, and we take this stuff, then aren't we looters?"

Dad narrowed his eyes. "What makes you say that?"

I shrugged. "The soldiers at the school said looters would be shot on sight."

Dad shook his head. "We are not looting. We are rescuing this food before it is lost to the snow. We would never loot, OK?"

"OK."

IT HAD BEEN strange watching the houses in our neighborhood grow shorter and shorter until all the windows on the ground floor were gone, and only the tops of the upper floors were visible.

After what happened at the Lawrence's, Dad boarded up our first-floor windows with thick scaffolding planks to stop the weight of the snow pushing them in. He boarded up the second-floor windows before the snow covered them, too. I helped by holding the long wood nails for him while he pounded each heavy wooden plank into place.

"It'll keep the house a little warmer, too," he said between nailing planks.

Now, it was dark inside the house, even during the day. But not the regular kind of dark. Instead, it was like a bunch of cold, gray shadows had moved in, turning everything into outlines, so you had to be careful when you walked around.

Dad and I were up on the roof the following week, cleaning the snow off the solar panels. They had to be cleaned every day to prevent ice from forming and blocking sunlight from getting to the panels or, worse, damaging them. I was brushing snow off one of the panels when I spotted something in the distance.

Pointing, I called Dad, "There's smoke over there."

The sky was a brilliant blue. Looking at it made me shiver, knowing it meant more freezing weather was on the way. Dad paused, broom in hand, face pink with cold, and squinted across the strange landscape of snow-covered roofs.

"That's interesting," he said, scrutinizing the column of smoke. "I didn't think anyone stayed on in our neighborhood. Everyone evacuated on the Army trucks or drove out by themselves. I wonder who that could be?"

I watched the smoke snake up into the sky. It looked to be a mile or two away. Such a distance would have been a half-hour walk before the snow. Now, it was half a day's journey with snowshoes.

We had seen no sign of anyone else since we had tried to take Mr Barnes to the hospital. Although Dad's truck was safe in the garage, the entrance to the garage was buried under twenty feet of snow. It would be impossible to clear a path for the truck. And what would be the point, with the roads under a similar depth of snow? If people were living nearby, we might never know, unless we looted their house.

Staring at the curling ribbon of sooty black smoke, I had a sudden bad feeling.

"Dad," I said, "Don't go and check it out."

Dad looked at me in surprise. "Why not?"

"Please. Just don't. What if it's him, the man from the hospital?"

Dad laughed. "That weekend warrior?" But he must have seen how serious I looked because he added, "There's no way that man could make it all the way here. Not under these conditions."

"He said it wasn't safe anywhere anymore."

"He was right on that score," Dad said brightly. "In this snow, you need to be careful. Sink into it somewhere, and you might never be able to dig yourself out again."

I watched Dad. I could tell from the look in his eye he knew I knew the man with the shotgun had not meant anything about snow. He had been referring to people. I didn't call Dad out on the lie because I knew he had told it to cheer me up. Instead, I said, "Don't worry about me. I'm like a fox. I can dig myself out of any snow hole."

Dad grunted a skeptical grunt, and we returned to cleaning the solar panels.

Later, when we were inside and sitting in the kitchen with Mom, drinking steaming mugs of milky hot chocolate (made with canned condensed milk; I preferred condensed milk, Johnny Ray did not), Dad said, "We've seen wolf tracks, haven't we, Austin?"

I nodded, watching Dad over the rim of my mug, before adding, "Big paw prints" for Johnny Ray's benefit.

"Wolves?" Johnny Ray wailed. "Are there wolves? I'm scared of wolves!"

"Now, see what you've done," Mom scolded Dad. "You've frightened Johnny Ray." She put her arm around him to soothe him.

"Since when were you frightened of wolves?" Dad asked the quaking Johnny Ray. "I thought the wolf enclosure at the zoo was your favorite exhibit."

"That was when they were on the inside, not the outside," Johnny Ray shot back, clinging to Mom's arm.

Dad and I looked at each other. Johnny Ray was right. That's where the wolves came from. With the snow piled up so high, they likely walked straight out of their enclosure over the top of the fence.

I said, "This snowy weather would be perfect for the wolves in the zoo."

Later that night, after we had gone to bed and I was supposed to be asleep, I heard Mom and Dad arguing quietly in the Games Room.

"I want you to keep your father's revolver loaded. Just in case."

There was a muffled response from Dad.

"I don't care. Keep it loaded. Where do you hide the key for the filing cabinet?"

There was another muffled response from Dad.

"Show me."

Dad grunted, and I heard him climb out of bed. There was the sound of metal-on-metal, high up in the ceiling, and the tinkle of a key ring.

"OK. At least the boys won't get up there."

I heard Dad climb back into bed, saying something in a complaining voice.

"That's just how it is now," Mom said bluntly. "One other thing. I think we should use the emergency satellite GPS signal, Daniel."

Again, Dad said something I could not hear.

"If you don't use it, I will," Mom threatened.

I lay there, staring up at the radiator pipes running along the ceiling joists, wondering what an emergency satellite GPS signal might bring.

JOHNNY RAY SAT up in bed and said, "I hear something."

I sat up, too, blinking in the dimness, and listened. I heard a low, distant rumbling.

"Wow," Johnny Ray said, more as a question than an exclamation. The world outside had been free of artificial sound since the last Army trucks had rumbled away. And now there was this…noise. A big noise, but still far away.

Johnny Ray clambered out of bed, stepping on me in the rush.

"Hey!" I complained, taking a swipe at him and missing.

"It's getting louder!"

He was right. It was.

"Come on!" He pulled on a hoodie and pants over his pajamas.

I slid from the warmth of the bedcovers and started dressing, too.

Dad's sleepy voice came from the Games Room. "What's going on, boys?"

"Can't you hear it, Dad?!" Johnny Ray called, bouncing up and down in excitement.

We didn't wait for a reply. We ran upstairs through the first and second floors, dark from the boarded-up windows and full of menacing shadows. Then we clambered up the narrow stairs to the attic. The attic was awash with morning's grey light. We couldn't see anything through the skylight, even though the sound was much louder now.

"Quickly, let's get our gear on," I instructed Johnny Ray. We charged back downstairs, pulled on coats and hats, and once I had my snow boots on, I helped Johnny Ray with his. "OK, back up. Onto the roof."

In the attic, I used the hook to pull down the ladder for the skylight, which, once opened, gave us access to the roof. The sky was as gray as lead and full of snow. The sound was more unmistakable up here, a powerful thrumming *whop-whop-whop* noise.

"It's a helicopter," I said, scanning the sky and seeing only swirling snow.

"Helicopter," Johnny Ray repeated, eye gleaming. "Can we get higher? I can't see anything."

In the roof valley, our view of the sky was limited. We were not supposed to climb higher because of the danger of falling into the snow. Mom had been strict on this point, even though falling off the roof looked fun, with the snow piled up to the top of the bedroom windows. However, she had insisted, saying we could be buried and suffocate.

The air was starting to vibrate with the noise of the rotor blades.

"It must be one big ol' 'copter," Johnny Ray shouted.

I bit my lip. I did not want to miss it. Maybe we could wave to the pilot. Let him know we were here.

"OK. Follow me and be careful. Don't stand on the flat side of the solar panels, only the edges."

We used the panels to get up to the ridgeline. Johnny Ray plumped himself down on the top, using his mitten'd hands and knees to grip either side of the ridge. I kneeled behind him, close enough to grab him if he slipped.

The noise was so loud that Johnny Ray, turning this way and that, had to yell to be heard. "Where is it? Where is it?"

Dad's head appeared through the skylight. He looked around and saw us and waved, shouting something. We couldn't hear anything over the thunder of the still-invisible helicopter. He clambered up into the roof valley and followed our path to the ridge. Putting his head close to mine, he yelled, "You boys should not be up here!"

That was when the helicopter materialized out of the gray.

It was a huge black thing hovering to the right of, and above, our location, over where the road used to be. It was making an enormous noise, battering the air and whipping the snow into violently twisting eddies and mini-tornados.

"Chinook! Chinook!" I screamed, recognizing the fore-and-aft arrangement of lift rotors, the elongated body, and the landing wheels on the ends of their bow-legged struts, but my words were swallowed in the all-enveloping roar.

After a moment that seemed to stretch forever, the machine rose and disappeared as if by magic.

We all looked up, mouths open, stunned.

There was a motion in the corner of my eye. Mom appeared in the skylight, gesturing frantically. I stared at her, still deaf from the helicopter roar. Dad saw her, too, and waved back. She pointed up into the sky, pointed, and waved, wanting Dad to attract the helicopter's attention. Dad nodded and waved back, showing he had understood. Then she gestured at me to come down from the ridgeline and bring Johnny Ray.

I shook my head. I could not miss this, not for the world.

She climbed out of the skylight, looking angry and determined.

The huge *whop-whop-whop* noise faded. Then grew.

Dad was looking this way and that, trying to locate the source of the noise.

Johnny Ray saw Mom and the expression on her face, put his mouth close to my ear, and yelled, "Do we have to go?"

I opened my mouth to reply, but the words were pummeled off the tip of my tongue by the helicopter, which materialized out of the sky directly above us.

The downdraft slammed into me, making a blinding blizzard of the snow and knocking Johnny Ray clean off the ridgeline. He slid down the roof, on his back, over the solar panels, and straight into Mom's arms, where she had rushed to catch him. I lay flat on the hump of the ridge, digging my mitten'd hands into the snow until I could grip the roof tiles underneath. I was holding on for dear life and trying to protect my face from the stinging snow and ice crystals ripping through the air. Even Dad was kneeling, his arms over his head, protecting himself from the battering we were being subjected to.

The enormous sound of the rotors oscillated strangely. Out of a half-closed, squinting eye, I saw the helicopter wobble and veer sideways, stabilize for a moment, and then one end dipped, so the machine was tilted up at an odd, dangerous-looking angle. At that point, it started sliding backward through the falling snow, low, much too low, over the snow-covered roofs of the houses opposite before the storm swallowed it up. The *whop-whop-whop* continued, a different sound, higher, more frantic like the rotors were clawing at the air, and then there was a visceral *whump*. I felt as much as I heard the noise, as if something very heavy had hit the ground, hard. The rotors stopped in the same instant, and we were left in the silence of the falling snow.

I picked myself up and wiped the snow from my face and eyes. "Did it land? Did it land?" I called Dad, my voice urgent and afraid for the pilots and the helicopter.

He looked at me, his face a mask of distress, and I could see his mouth moving, but I was still half-deaf from the noise of the helicopter's rotors.

Still holding Johnny Ray, Mom called to Dad, "Go and see, go and see. They must have got the signal. They must have come for us!"

I thought: She couldn't have seen how the helicopter slid sideways into the storm.

Dad said, "Yes, yes. Let me get some things together first. Then I'll go."

"Why? Why wait?" Mom asked, sounding confused and frustrated.

We climbed down through the skylight into the attic.

"Just in case."

Finally, Mom seemed to register the expression on Dad's face. "Do you think..." she said, and then she saw him glance at Johnny Ray and me and said, "Just be quick. The last thing we want is for them to fly away without us."

He said nothing to that.

I watched him put the emergency medical kit in his backpack before hoisting it over his shoulder, pulling on his snow goggles and snowshoes, and climbing off the roof onto the snow.

"Can I come, Dad?" I asked.

He shook his head. "Not this time. You stay behind and look after Mom and Johnny Ray."

As soon as Dad was gone, Mom had us repack our suitcases. We had packed them once already when she thought we were going to leave with the evacuation, and then we'd unpack them when we did not.

"Here, Johnny Ray," she said, "I'll help you." And, to me, "Be sure to take all your school books. I guarantee you will have an absolute mountain of schoolwork to catch up on. Life will be truly miserable if you forget those. Trousers, under-pants, socks, T-shirts, hoodies. And at least two pairs of shoes. No cold-weather gear. What you are wearing will be enough. Choose only your favorite toys. Alright?"

I nodded and clumped into my bedroom with my suitcase hanging open and dragging behind me.

I didn't dare ask her what the point of this exercise was, given it was clear the helicopter must have crash-landed. And if it had, it wouldn't be flying anytime soon. Mom had gotten it into her head we were going to leave right away, and noth-ing, not even a crashed helicopter, would stop her from getting us ready. I had visions of her making us walk back to civilization on our snowshoes, dragging the suitcases in a pile behind us on top of the big green sled.

I heaved the suitcase onto the bed and grabbed random handfuls of clothes from the chest of drawers. I threw in four shoes I pulled out of the closet, not even bothering to check if they were pairs. Looking at my schoolbooks, I was struck down by a treacly lethargy. I had to sit on the bed and compose myself, exhaling clouds of steam in the freezing air. Slouched there, I stared at my toy collection and signed. Picking just a few was impossible. I bet Mom would be taking all her toiletries. My eye alighted on the Lego Millennium Falcon I had "rescued" from Jamie Lawrence's bedroom when we had "rescued" the cans and packets of food from their house. Taking it had been a mistake, and now it couldn't be undone. Dad had left Jamie's bedroom window open. The room was filled to the ceiling with drifting snow. All his toys would be encased in ice.

I picked up the model. It was a handsome thing — an object of beauty. I made a sour face. I bet he hadn't rebuilt it by himself. His Dad must have helped him. I imagined them trying to figure out how to reassemble the Lego model with all the unique pieces. Then I looked at the box with the heap of Lego that had been my cheap, cobbled-together Millennium Falcon, long abandoned.

I took his model, wrapped it in a couple of hoodies, and placed it in the suitcase, packing clothes around. There was no room for anything else, especially the school books. I hid them under the bed, shoving them as far out of sight as possible.

Mom would understand when I explained.

On cue, Mom called, "Are you done yet?" from Johnny Ray's room.

"Yes!" I yelled back.

"If I check your suitcase, will everything I asked for be there?" she demanded.

"Yes!" I yelled back.

"Good!" she yelled, sounding as annoyed as I was.

I placed the suitcase by the door. I didn't want to stay in my bedroom any longer. The strange feelings and weird memories were too much. Instead, I climbed up into the attic and, through the skylight, onto the roof, walking to the end of the valley to glimpse Dad. His tracks had already disappeared under the new-fallen snow.

"Do you see him?" Mom asked softly, coming up behind me and putting her gloved hands on my shoulders.

"No," I said, unable to shed the peculiar mood gripping me.

"I hope he comes back soon. It's getting late."

"I should go and check he's OK," I said, still irritated with her.

"No. That's very brave of you, but Dad will be OK."

During dinner, we heard Dad's footsteps on the roof and descending into the attic. Johnny Ray and I abandoned our food and went racing upstairs.

"Dad! Dad! Did you see the helicopter, Dad? Did you?" Johnny Ray jumped up and down while Dad knocked the snow off his boots and clothes into the bath.

"I was getting worried," Mom said, coming up behind us and watching Dad with a half-concerned, half-quizzical look. "You were out a long time. It's almost dark."

He looked utterly frozen. "I need something to drink."

I knew immediately he'd seen the helicopter.

So did Mom.

WE DIDN'T TALK about the Chinook after that. My suitcase sat by my bedroom door, gathering the snow that swirled in through the attic skylight whenever we went in and out. The drifts were getting higher, covering the eaves of the roof.

Mom and Dad had been insulating the basement, lining the walls with mattresses we had "rescued" from neighboring houses, covering them with plastic sheeting to hold them in place, and stuffing the gaps in between with bedding.

Mom fretted over the carbon monoxide alarm, which she

had started checking obsessively. "What if we run out of batteries?"

"We won't," Dad reassured her.

We collected firewood. Dad would break up furniture in the surrounding houses, and Mom and me would haul it back on the sled. A pile of it was in the living room.

"Burns too fast," Mom complained as we huddled around the fire.

Dad said he would cut down tree branches. Cutting branches was easy, as the snowdrifts were pretty much at the height of the branches. It was new wood, Dad said, "Burns wet," and it did, hissing and bubbling in the fireplace, along with the bed slats, chair legs, and coffee tables we threw on.

"I want schmoes!" Johnny Ray complained, folding his arms across his chest in protest, the firelight reflecting orangey-red on his face.

Mom and Dad just laughed.

I didn't say anything. But I sure wanted schmoes, too.

Mom was careful using the cooker. The first big propane gas tank was finished, and Dad connected the stove to the second one. "After that, it's going to be salad for dinner every night," he joked.

No-one laughed.

We had started having our hot chocolate with more water than condensed milk and less hot chocolate power, so it was more like drinking brown-colored water than hot chocolate. At least it was hot. I began exploring houses a little further away, hoping to find more chocolate and condensed milk. Mom made me take Johnny Ray with me on these trips to get him out from under her and Dad's feet. Johnny Ray was a real pain to explore with. He was slow, and he got tired, and then he spent all his time complaining, saying he wanted to go home.

On this expedition, he decided to sit in the snow and refuse to move.

"Look, maybe we can find marshmallows."

Johnny Ray huffed, light feathery snowflakes settling on him. I thought, *If I leave him and go on, he'll be forced to follow.* But, knowing him, he would sit right there, like a pint-sized garden Buddha, the snow covering him until he'd be a snowy lump among all the other snowy lumps, and I'd never find him again.

"If we find chocolate bars, you know what we can make, right?"

His interest perked up. "Schmoes?"

"Yeah. What d'you think of that?"

"Let's go!"

We trudged on, two be-goggled explorers in a surreal winter wilderness, looking for a house we had not yet broken into. We'd find a window on the lee side of the building, sheltered from the wind. I would use the heel of my snowshoe to smash the glass, reach in and release the latch, and heave the window open. Then, I'd bundled Johnny Ray inside and climb in after him.

In this house, we didn't bother with the bedrooms, only the kitchen. Descending to the first floor was eerie. The light faded into a gray, shadowy dimness full of ghosts. Johnny Ray stuck so close to me that we kept bumping into each other. The open plan downstairs provided sufficient light for our kitchen search. I rummaged through the cupboards while Johnny Ray kept repeating, "Can we go now?" I found a pot of Nutella spread, some honey, and four cans of condensed milk. "Gold mine!" I said to the darkness. Johnny Ray chipped in with, "*Now,* can we go?"

I stuffed our haul into my backpack, and we headed back into the daylight.

"One more house," I told Johnny Ray, "I'm feeling lucky."

"For marshmallows?" He asked, perking up.

"You got it!"

We clambered around a roof poking out of a snowdrift, and there it was.

The Chinook.

It was upside down, the rear end pointing up at the sky. The cockpit was buried somewhere far below. The tip of one of the big rear rotor blades was sticking straight up out of the snow like the mast of a ship.

"Wow," Johnny Ray said. "It crashed."

"Didn't you know?"

"No," Johnny Ray said, marveling at the wreckage.

The rear entrance to the interior has collapsed, leaving a gaping hole in the fuselage.

"Let's have a look. See if we can see anything."

I moved closer, Johnny Ray following me at a distance.

I edged up to the fuselage opening. It was like the entrance to a metal cave. Dark and full of stuff covered in snow, I couldn't make any sense of it.

"Are there dead people in there?" Johnny-Ray demanded.

"I don't know," I said. I hadn't thought of that. I slipped my goggles onto my forehead and stared down into the interior of the wrecked helicopter, straining my eyes. There were seats on the ceiling. Was something hanging from one of them?

"Look, there's footprints!"

I tuned to see where Johnny Ray was pointing. Tracks led away from the helicopter. They looked like a person's tracks. Even as we watched, the snow began to cover them up.

There was a scrabbling sound from within the helicopter, claws on metal.

I jumped — and I mean *jumped* — and scooted back to where Johnny Ray was standing. He was looking at me, wide-eyed. "What was that?"

"You heard it, too?"

He nodded.

"I don't know," I said.

My heart was pounding, and my breath was coming fast. I looked back at the upside-down entrance to the wrecked Chinook.

"We gotta go," Johnny Ray said, tugging at my arm.

"Yeah, let's go."

We snowshoed back the way we had come, Johnny Ray in front. The snowfall was thick and heavy, making it difficult to follow our old snowshoe prints.

"What's that?" Johnny Ray hissed. He was looking off to our left. I searched with my eyes where he pointed, but I couldn't see anyone or anything, just the strange Dr Seuss shapes of the snow-covered house roofs and treetops.

"What did it look like?"

"Someone," Johnny Ray said.

"Like a man? Nothing else?"

Johnny-Ray nodded.

I let my breath out. At least it wasn't…whatever was inside the Chinook. The tracks by the helicopter were recent. Maybe…

"We better get home," I said.

Johnny Ray said, "Yeah, we better."

THAT NIGHT, we had Nutella and condensed milk in our hot chocolate, and it was good. (Although the Nutella did leave a film of oil on the hot chocolate.)

Johnny Ray could not keep his mouth shut. He was happy as punch, sitting by the fire, the furniture burning up a storm and the logs sizzling, sap bubbling out of their unburnt ends. He said, "We saw the 'copter, Dad."

I gave him a laser-beam stare and kicked him with my booted foot.

He shrugged off the assault.

"Really?" Dad said. Then, looking at me, "You walked all that way?"

I shrugged. "We were looking for marshmallows."

"Hmph," Dad said.

Mom said, "You shouldn't be wandering far from the house, especially with Johnny Ray. What if he fell into a snow-hole?"

"I'd pull him out," I said.

"What if you both fell into a snow-hole?"

"I'd..."

"Don't talk back to your mother, Austin," Dad warned.

"I wasn't," I said, offended.

"The point stands. Don't stray too far from home."

We sat, drinking our hot chocolate Nutella mix. Then Johnny Ray opened his big mouth again. "There was something inside the 'copter."

Dad nodded. "Was there, now?"

"Yes, yes! There was!" Johnny Ray's eyes got large as he stared into the fire, "It was..." he paused for dramatic effect. "A *monster*."

"Really?" Dad said. "You saw this monster?"

"No, but we saw someone else."

Startled, Dad looked up from the book he was trying to read by the firelight. "You saw someone?"

I shook my head. "I didn't see anyone."

"I did, I did!" Johnny Ray insisted.

"Are you sure?" Dad asked.

"Yes, yes! We saw tracks."

Dad turned to me. "Is that right, Austin?"

I gave Johnny Ray another death-ray stare and nodded.

"Why didn't you tell me?"

I shrugged, "I dunno."

"Always tell me or Mom know about anything unusual, OK?"

Johnny Ray and I both nodded.

Mom said, "Could it be someone searching for the Chinook?"

Dad said, "Maybe. Let's see."

"DAD! DAD! COME UP, COME UP!"

Johnny Ray was shouting down through the skylight.

I was with Mom in the kitchen while Dad was checking the furnace down in the basement. Mom sighed, "Austin, please go and see what all the fuss is about."

"OK."

I scrambled up through the skylight. Johnny Ray was crouched on the ridgeline, peaking over the top of the roof.

"What is it?" I called up to him.

"Something," he said in a hushed voice. "Come and see."

"It better be real," I warned. I clambered up the solar panels and lay beside him, peering over the ridge. Snow and snow-covered roofs dazzled in the sunlight.

"Where?" I asked.

Johnny Ray pointed at a depression in the snow, marking the gap between two houses opposite.

"I don't see anything, Johnny Ray."

"Wait," he said, staring with great intensity at the spot.

Lying there, enjoying the sun's warmth, I wondered if this was the start of the thaw. Dad said the jet stream couldn't stay stalled forever. At some point (not too soon, I hoped), the snow would disappear, and there would be "one hell of a thaw." I tried to imagine all this snow thawing. It would be wild. What would happen when people returned to the houses we had broken into and "rescued" stuff from them? I winced.

"There!" Johnny-Ray hissed.

In a heartbeat, I was back in the present.

"Did you see it?"

I squinted. "Maybe." I had seen something like a shadow from the corner of my eye. "Wait here. I'll go and get Dad."

Dad kneeled in front of the furnace in the basement, cleaning the burners. "If we waste less fuel, we stay warmer longer," he informed me.

"Johnny Ray has seen something across the street."

Dad wiped his sooty-black hands on a rag. "Did he say what it was?"

"No."

"Did you see it?"

"I think so."

"What was it?"

"I don't know. I only caught a glimpse of it."

Dad considered, looking at me speculatively. "Well, I better come and have a look, I suppose. Let me get the binoculars."

Johnny Ray was on the roof at his sentry post, eyes fixed on the spot he'd seen something.

We climbed up beside him.

"Well, where is it, Hawk-Eye?" Dad asked.

"There," Johnny Ray whispered, pointing.

Dad put the binoculars to his eyes and studied the gap. "Hmmm." He scanned the binoculars back and forth, adjusting the focus. "I might see something." He scanned some more, then said, "You're right. There are tracks; there, by that roof."

"See, I was right!" Johnny Ray hissed, giving me snake eyes.

"I didn't say you were wrong," I shot back.

Dad put down the binoculars. "Shush, you two." Then, frowning, "Whomever it was kept themselves well hidden."

"Sneaking around," Johnny Ray said in an accusatory tone.

"It must be the person you saw visiting the helicopter," Dad said. "I wonder what he or she is up to?"

Behind us, someone said, "Don't move."

We all turned, startled.

A man stood at the far end of the roof valley. The snow had piled there, allowing him to walk, unheard, onto the roof behind us. He was dressed in camouflaged combat gear and carrying a shotgun. He pointed the gun at Dad.

I recognized him and the gun from the hospital.

The weekend warrior.

My stomach went cold, and I felt sick.

"You," he was looking at Dad. "Come down, slowly." He nodded to the other end of the roof valley. "Bring the boys with you. Carefully, now. Nice and slow, no sudden moves. One shot from the shotgun will hurt you all, bad. That's it, that's it. Stop right there. Now, get down on your stomachs and put your hands on your heads." Johnny Ray and I watched Dad kneel and lie down at the bottom of the valley. He put his hands behind his head, forcing him to rest his face on the snow. "You boys, just like your father." We lay down, too, behind Dad. My face was resting in the snow, like Dad's. The snow made my skin burn. I could hear Johnny Ray fussing and spitting and then complaining, "It's too cold."

The man said, "Best be quiet, lest you want me to shoot your Pop." Johnny Ray went quiet. "Good. Now, stay like that. Don't move, and everything will be OK."

By tilting my head, I could see the man stepping over to the skylight and peering into the attic. "Who else is down in there? No lies. I been watching your house. If someone surprises me, I'll shoot 'em first, ask questions later."

"Someone's in the kitchen," Dad said, lying face down in the snow.

"Who's in the kitchen?"

Dad hesitated, then said, almost defiantly, "My wife."

"Yeah. Good for you, you didn't lie. I hate lairs. I know who all lives here. I been watching you. Cozy little setup you got here. Solar. Propane stove. Oil-burning furnace, too, I reckon. The envy of the neighborhood, buddy. Envy of the neighborhood. You," he pointed the gun at me, "Go and get your pretty little mommy up here. Nothing funny, right? Yeah?"

I nodded.

"You love your little brother and your Poppy, right? So you don't want to do nothing that might get 'em hurt," and he waved the shotgun toward Dad and Johnny Ray, who was lying against Dad's legs.

"No," I said and looked at Dad.

He smiled at me. "Do what the man says. Here, walk past me."

Dad rolled to the side so I could step by him. As I did so, he took his hand from his head, put the knuckle against his cheek, and sighted down his finger like he was sighting down a gun. Before the weekend warrior could see the gesture, Dad changed it into one where he was wiping away snow stuck to his face.

The weekend warrior backed away from the skylight, keeping the gun trained on me as I climbed down into the darkness.

As soon as I was out of sight, I raced to the kitchen. It was empty.

"Mom!" I hissed. "Mom, where are you!?"

The living room and dining room were both empty. She must be in the basement. I hurried down the stairs, looking in the Games Room and toilet. Still, I couldn't find her.

My heart was galloping like it was fit to bust. I felt dizzy, confused, and frantic. Where had she gone? Then I heard her on the second floor above me, calling up to Dad. If she poked her head out of the skylight, the man would shoot her in the face! I raced back up the basement stairs and was halfway up the main stairs when a scream pierced the air.

I froze.

I could hear Mom begging. The man was speaking like he

was angry. Feet moved about on the roof. My heart raced a hundred miles an hour, yet I felt icy cold. I had seen Dad sight down his finger. I knew what he wanted me to do: Warn Mom to get the gun. Somehow, I had missed her, and now she was trapped on the roof, too.

I listened, straining to hear what was going on.

The man was saying something. Mom was saying, "No, no, no, no," in a desperate voice.

I stood motionless, gritting my teeth and cursing Mom for not being in the kitchen.

What was I supposed to do now?

I had to get the gun to Mom or Dad somehow.

Turning back, I crept down the stairs, along the hall to the basement door, and down into the Games Room. Mom and Dad's bed filled most of the space. The foosball table had been stacked on top of the washing machine. The filing cabinet was shoved into the corner by the basement toilet. I tried the drawer containing the gun. It was locked. I bit my lip, thinking about all the times I'd listened to Dad open the filing cabinet. He did something high up, like he hid the key in the ceiling somewhere. I glanced at the jumble of pipes above me. I had to get up there. Clambering onto the top of the filing cabinet, I reached for a heating pipe. Gripping it, I pulled myself up until my head was above the pipework. There was dust and shadows everywhere. I squinted. And saw the key. It hung from a bracket over on the other side of the room. I jumped down from the cabinet onto the bed, scooped up a pillow, and used it to try and knock the key off the bracket. It came down on the third attempt. I grabbed it and fumbled it into the lock on the filing cabinet. The drawer slid open, and there was the revolver.

I reached in and pulled the gun out. It seemed bigger and felt heavier than I remembered, weighing down my whole arm. Holding it by the grip and keeping my finger away from the trigger, I ran up the basement stairs and tiptoed up the main stairs to the attic stairs.

And listened.

Mom was talking. Her voice sounded strained. She was saying something about children, but I couldn't hear what.

I edged up the attic stairs and tiptoed to the skylight ladder. There was no sign of the weekend warrior above. I could hear Mom more clearly now. She sounded like she was with Dad and Johnny Ray at the far end of the roof valley. Craning my head, I could glimpse the top of the weekend warrior's head.

I climbed the ladder, gripping the gun. My head came level with the top of the skylight. The weekend warrior was standing ten feet from me. He was facing Mom, his back to me. Dad and Johnny Ray were lying face down in the snow. There was no way I could get the gun to Mum or Dad.

What was I supposed to do?

I felt tears of frustration prickle my eyes.

Mom was kneeling by Dad and Johnny Ray. She was clutching her hands in prayer and pleading with the man, who was pointing the shotgun straight at her.

"I beg you, let them go. You can have me. Do whatever you want. I don't care as long as you let them go. Let them walk off. They have done nothing to you, they…"

The weekend warrior cut her off. "He saw us cutting up that nurse. He knows what was going on. He knows me. I cain't let him walk off. And anyways, what's to stop him coming back?"

"For the life of my child." Mom put her hand tenderly on Johnny Ray's head. I could hear him whimpering, crying softly into the snow. "We will give you anything for the life of my child."

I raised the gun using both hands like I'd seen in the movies a thousand times. It weighed so fricking much! My arms were aching. Instead of being perfect, the revolver seemed clumsy and dangerous.

Mom saw me, caught my eye for a split second, and started talking urgently to the man. At the same time, she unzipped her jacket and then unbuttoned the top of her dress. "In a world like this, the man with the gun gets what he wants. You can have this." I pointed the gun at the weekend warrior's butt. "What's it worth if I'm dead? I want to live. You can have me if this is what it takes to stay alive."

I started to pull the trigger. Were there any bullets in the gun? I hadn't checked! Had Dad said he was going to leave it loaded? Or not? I couldn't remember…

"You can have me. Why not? It's a simple pleasure between two people." I shifted my finger to press the cylinder release. The cylinder slid out of the gun. There were bullets in three of the six chambers. Mom was showing the man her brassiere, pulling down one of the cups so he could see her breast. "I'm still young, still soft, still willing…"

I eased the cylinder back into the gun. It made a slight *click* as it seated home.

The man's head snapped around. He looked at me in shock and surprise. I saw him bring the muzzle of the shotgun around to point it into my face.

Mom let out an ear-piercing scream.

I pulled the trigger.

There was an explosion, and the world went black.

———

I WAS LYING in bed in the basement. Mom was sitting beside me, holding my hand. My face hurt, hurt bad, drawing a deep moan out of me. Only I didn't want to move my jaw or my head. Mom gripped my hand more tightly in hers.

"Stay still, Austin. No need to move. Take this. It'll help."

I felt her ease a pill between my lips, and it reminded me

of the way she had done the same thing for Mr Barnes. I panicked, shivering, and she said, "Calm down, calm down, it's just a painkiller, that's all. It will make you feel better."

I used my tongue to move the pill onto the roof of my mouth, and Mom moved her hand to the back of my head to raise it so she could put a cup of water to my lips. I did not want to move my face at all, but with her prompting, I opened my mouth ever so slightly, letting some of the water dribble onto my tongue to swallow the pill. Most of the water ran down my chin and onto my chest. On the third attempt, it went down, only to stick in my throat. I motioned for more water. Each swallow made me tremble with pain. Finally, the pill dislodged, and I could lay my head back on the pillow. Mom put my hand to her lips and kissed it.

The whole right side of my cheek felt caved in, as if someone had hit me in the face with a hammer.

The thought of my injury scared me, and I moaned, "Mom!" tears leaking from my eyes and into the bandages on my face. I experienced an intense, brittle fear, thinking I would die, while Mom held my hand.

Mom stroked my forehead. "Take it easy, Austin. You're OK. Don't worry. Everything is fine, everything is fine." Her voice was calm and steady, giving me reassurance and allowing me to contain my fear.

I closed my eyes, concentrating on trying to cope with the agony of my wounded face. The pain seemed to radiate from my nose and cheek. It was like a pincushion of red-hot needles had been pushed into the skin and bone below my eye. I didn't dare move because whenever I did, those needles sent burning white sparks of agony into my eye. I could taste blood on my teeth and feel the strapping and sticking plaster on my ear, neck, and chin. I gripped Mom's hand and made a low, continuous moaning sound in my throat until my throat hurt, and I had to give up.

I must have fallen asleep, waking up alone in the darkness,

crying out for Mom. In a moment, she was by my side, taking my hand and telling me everything was alright.

Having her there calmed me down. I breathed slowly, feeling the warmth of my hand in hers. The pain in my face was less. I could feel structure to the wound, areas where the skin burned and stung and the bone ached, a deep throbbing ache, and I knew I wasn't going to die. However, my face was going to be changed. I was going to be one ugly-looking kid. I don't know where this stray thought came from. It made me want to laugh. Only I couldn't. I started hiccuping and convulsing, trying not to laugh, and Mom panicked, calling Dad, who appeared beside her, looking down at me out of the darkness, a worried look on his face, which transformed to a frown and, then, a crooked grin. He knelt by the bed and lightly put his hand on my chest, asking, "What's so funny, Austin?"

I COULD WALK AROUND in a couple of days. The right side of my face was still covered in bandages and strapping, making me feel like an oddball supervillain from the movies: *Beware, Captain Bandage-Face Man!* (I was careful not to make myself laugh.)

Eating and drinking was a chore because I couldn't open my mouth, and I got sick of having soup all the time and even Nutella hot chocolate.

Johnny Ray was subdued around me. I would catch him examining my face from the corner of his eye as he pretended to do something else. He was sleeping in Mom and Dad's bed in the Games Room while I was recovering. He would play in there, too, when I was in the basement, leaving me alone. We were awkward in each other's company — I felt changed and apart from him.

I enjoyed being outside because of the cold.

The cold made the pain in my face less. Trolling around the neighboring houses, I could almost forget about it. I couldn't stay out very long because I couldn't put my goggles on — I couldn't bear anything touching my nose or cheek — and I got snow-blind and had to come back inside.

I discovered something interesting — a hole in the snow on the far side of Mr Barnes' house.

It was a big hole. Someone, or something, had dug it. Looking into it, I saw it led through a window into a second-floor room. Not Mr Barnes's bedroom, but the room diagonally opposite, equivalent to Johnny-Ray's bedroom in our house. Tracks led into the hole. Wolf paw-prints. Like the tracks we have seen before. They lead off along a path between the snow-covered roofs. I found some of their scat half hidden under an eave heavy with snow. I squatted down and examined it, remembering the sound of claws scrabbling on metal in the upside-down Chinook. As I looked, I noticed something poking out of the snow. I reached under the eave and pulled out a pair of long white bones. They were joined by a piece of gristle, with some smaller bones dangling from them.

They looked like part of a human arm.

Mom changed the dressing on my face every night. I hated having the dressing changed. She insisted the wounds had to be kept clean. Otherwise, they wouldn't get better. I insisted Johnny Ray play in the Games Room while Mom was tending to my face. He stared at me without the dressing as if I was some kind of a freak.

"Do I look bad?" I asked Mom while she was wiping anti-septic cream onto the scabs and crispy, flaking skin on the swollen bridge of my nose.

"No!" she said, frowning. "You look beautiful."

"Boys don't look beautiful."

"You do to me. Once healed, you will look very rugged

and handsome, I can assure you. Girls will be falling over each other to be your girlfriend."

I wanted to frown at her but couldn't move my face, so I shook my head. "I hate girls."

Mom laughed. "Really? You may revise your opinion a few years from now. But, let's see."

———

I HAD no memory of what happened on the roof. All I remember was the weekend warrior appearing out of nowhere, and holding the revolver, and how heavy it was. After that, nothing. Mom didn't say anything, and Dad didn't say anything, so I wasn't able to ask the question I wanted to ask. Instead, I got to brooding.

Dad noticed my brooding. He put his hand on my shoulder. "Johnny Ray is feeling lonely."

I shrugged. I didn't want to play with Johnny Ray. There was an invisible barrier between us. He was just a kid.

"We need food. Come foraging with me."

The way he spoke, I knew there was a reason he wanted me to come along.

I shrugged again. "Sure. If you want."

Dad found some colored transparent plastic from an old Christmas decoration and made an impromptu visor for me. He appeared from the skylight with a pump-action shotgun slung over his shoulder. When he saw me looking at it, his expression went blank, and I knew he knew I knew where the gun came from.

We trudged a long way, Dad pulling the big green sled. We passed the upside-down Chinook. Dad paused, pointing at paw-prints in the snow.

"Wolf tracks."

The paw prints weaved past looted houses where we — or

was it the weekend warrior? — had broken in, to "rescue" stuff.

We snowshoed in single file, Dad leading. The plastic of my visor was dark pink, making the snowbound world look like a cartoon.

Except for the shotgun.

"Why have you got that gun?"

Dad glanced over his shoulder. "In case we need to scare off those rascally wolves."

I knew he misunderstood me on purpose.

I didn't say anything.

We came to a large, square building buried in the snow. It looked familiar, but I couldn't say why. Dad climbed onto the flat roof, pulling me up after him. We walked along a well-trodden path, past some vent pipes and two blocky AC units, to a square grill. Dad took a screwdriver from his pack and, kneeling, used it to open the grill, placing it to one side.

"We're going in there?"

Dad nodded.

"It's dark," I observed, peering into the hole.

Dad took a torch from his pocket, clicked it on, and gave it to me. He took out a second one for himself.

"Where did you get these?" I asked, looking at the torch.

"Down there." He smiled. "It's Aladdin's Cave. Want to check it out?"

I studied Dad, then the hole. Aladdin's Cave? "Sure."

We climbed down a ladder. Dad went first, helped me down, then returned to replace the grill.

"Don't want our wolf friends paying a visit while we are here."

We were in a small room full of pipes and wires. Using the torch, Dad guided me through the darkened building, past an office and a restroom, down metal steps, and into a much larger space. It took me several seconds to realize where we were in the darkness.

"It's Jempson's Store," I said in surprise.

"Right, the first time. It's where I got your snowshoes."

I shook my head. "We shouldn't be in here."

Dad smiled. "We didn't break in. Someone else did. We are just borrowing things until we can pay for them. No stealing. So, nothing to worry about. Come with me."

Dad picked up something from a shelf as we walked along the aisles. "Well, look at this!" He handed me a can of chocolate powder. "Shall we take it?"

I considered the can, turning it around in the beam of my flashlight. "Yeah. Maybe take two?"

"Excellent idea."

"We need condensed milk, too."

"Yes, they have that."

We got six tins.

A thought occurred to me. "They have marshmallows here."

Dad nodded. "I believe they do."

I left Dad hunting through the tinned vegetables while I searched the aisles for candy. I got turned around in the dark, confused by entering the store from the back. Panic rose in my throat, but I stayed calm. I switched off my flashlight and looked for the glow of Dad's light. There it was at the other end of the store. I breathed a sigh and turned my flashlight back on. I found the candy aisle and bags full of marshmallows. They looked OK. It was cold in the store, like a fridge, which must have helped preserve everything. I found some chocolate bars and stuffed everything into my backpack.

Dad had to go up and down the ladder multiple times to bring out the stuff we had collected from the store. While he did that, I stacked the cans, packets, and boxes on the big green sled. When he finished, he screwed the grill back in place and sat down beside me.

"Hungry? Yes? OK. Time for lunch."

Mom had made us sandwiches, and Dad had taken fizzy

drink cans from the store. I ate carefully because of the plasters over my cheek and nose and chewed slowly, but the food sure tasted good after all the work we'd been doing.

I squinted at the candies "rescued" from the store. "Can I have a marshmallow, too?"

Dad nodded. "We still have walking and hauling to do, so it's important to have energy."

I opened a packet, took a handful of soft, fluffy pink-and-white cubes, and wolfed them down. They tasted delicious, the best thing in the world. However, I had to stop after a while because they made me feel sick.

"All good?"

I nodded and belched a sugary marshmallow-flavored belch. All that sugar was making me feel light-headed. Then I saw the shotgun leaning against the sled and remembered the weekend warrior.

"What happened up on the roof, Dad?"

Dad made his face into a smile. Then he looked away over the snow-covered roofs.

"You firing Grandpa's revolver sure scared him." He nodded as if to confirm his own words and then looked back at me before looking away again.

"He fell right over. He fell right over and hit his head on the edge of the skylight. A very nasty knock." Dad tapped his temple with his finger and shook his head. "On the sharp corner of the skylight." He rubbed his thumb against his finger like he was trying to remove a stain. "It was a nasty fall. He wasn't expecting the bang that old gun made. Nor were you. The recoil hit you smack in the face, and you fell right off the ladder. The gun went off again when you hit the floor, whacking you in the face a second time. We came rushing down, and you were covered in so much blood, we thought you'd shot yourself, but you'd only put a hole in the attic wall." He laughed uncomfortably.

Then, in a rush, he said, looking straight at me, "But, you

know he shouldn't have been on our roof in the first place threatening us like he did. We didn't invite him up there, and he was pointing his gun around, and he scared Mom and Johnny Ray, and you can't do that on someone's property. No, siree, Bob, you can't. So, what you did," he looked away again, down at his hand, with the imaginary stain on it that wouldn't go away, "was the right thing, scaring him off our property. He wouldn't have fallen over and hit his head if he hadn't been there. That was his fault; it had nothing to do with you."

"Where is he now?" I asked, feeling my throat tighten.

Dad shrugged.

Dad never shrugged.

"That blow to his head. Well, it knocked him clean out. We were looking after you. And he scared us so much that we just left him there. When we came back, he was gone."

"Where did he go?"

"I don't know, Austin."

"Which way did his tracks go?"

Dad stared at me momentarily, an uncomfortable look on his face as if he hadn't thought about tracks.

"Well," he said, "I guess the snow must have covered them."

"It was sunny. No snow."

Dad shrugged again, and his gaze slipped away from mine, over the roofs.

"Is that why you have the pump-action shotgun, in case we meet him?"

Dad didn't shrug and didn't say anything.

We made schmoes that night by the fire. Johnny Ray was ecstatic, his chocolate-smeared face bright in the firelight. I didn't want any. I remembered feeling sick on top of Jempson's store, my stomach full of marshmallows, wishing I hadn't eaten even a single one of them.

Mom cleaned my wounds, changed the dressing, and

declared I would survive after all. She showed me the injuries in the mirror. My nose was crooked with a knot in it, and there was a long, lumpy red welt below my right eye. "You'll have a nice scar. Girls love scars," she said mischievously.

"Mom!" I complained.

———————

THE NEXT MORNING, I was up before anyone else.

Johnny Ray was still sleeping with Mom and Dad. He didn't want to come back and sleep with me, so I didn't have to worry about waking him, which suited me because I didn't want him around.

I got dressed and crept up to the attic. Looking around the walls, I found the bullet hole from the second shot when I fell off the ladder. The hole was bigger than I imagined, ragged around the edges, a scattering of plaster still on the floor. There was a sizeable irregular stain at the foot of the skylight ladder. It was black and looked like dried blood.

I climbed up to the skylight, unlatched it, and swung it open. On the roof, I examined the corner where Dad had said the man had struck his head. There was no damage to the frame or any trace of blood. I walked to the spot near the skylight where the man had been. No way could he have fallen forward and hit his head on the skylight.

I noticed a dimple in the snow. Leaning on the roof angle, I removed a mitten and carefully dug under the dimple. My fingers encountered something small and hard and jagged. I pulled it out and cleaned the snow off it. It was a small, slightly curved piece of bone with two teeth poking out of it. It was crusted black. It took me a moment to realize what it was. Revulsed, I hurled it away, as far as possible, into the trees behind the house. Then, I rubbed my hand vigorously on my jacket to clean them.

As I tried to rid my fingers of the slippery feel of the piece of jawbone, I noticed something was watching me.

There, across the expanse of snow, was a grey wolf. It stood tall, with broad shoulders, head turned, eyes fixed on me. It had something in its mouth. I wanted to see what it was. Was it a piece of clothing with a camouflage pattern on it? With something inside the clothing? But the cloud was low, and the light was murky. Another snowstorm was on the way.

A long, drawn-out howl brought the wolf's ears to points. It glanced toward the sound, then moved off at a steady lope, throwing up little puffs of snow.

END

Epilogue

WHAT IS the purpose of childhood?

Children are immature individuals who are highly vulnerable, due to both their ignorance and limited motor skills, as well as to direct threats in their environment (which potentially includes their parents, depending on the species — filial cannibalism is seen in hamsters, polar bears, and lions, for example). Offspring are, to a lesser or greater extent, a burden on their parents, depending on the level of parental care in the species in question, limiting their parents' productivity and potentially putting parents at an evolutionary disadvantage.

For humans, this period of childhood immaturity last a long time, relatively speaking, generally twice as long as our nearest relatives, the monkeys, among whom the orangutan has the longest childhood of all non-human animals, between 8-12 years. Furthermore, for humans, the notional period of childhood seems to be lengthening into young adulthood, so that it now extends through the late teens and early 20s and sometimes beyond, as defined by dependency on their parents.

From an evolutionary perspective, it would make sense to have childhood be as short as possible, reducing this period of vulnerability, minimizing the burden on parents, and generating a useful and productive member of society as quickly as possible.

Evolution has had roughly 4 billion years to sample the many tricks necessary to navigate an organism's developmental transition from immaturity to maturity — in essence, childhood to adulthood. Most of us have seen images of newborn gazelles, almost immediately up on their feet and wobbling around for the first time ever, and yet mere moments later, able to walk, and then run with their mothers, capable of hiding and avoiding predators. It takes a human baby from 9 to 17 months to be able to walk, and even longer before a child can be trusted to be independently mobile, let alone hide itself from predators.

In humans, this long period of childhood could be an advantage in and of itself, or, at least, the advantages could outweigh the disadvantages. However, a more likely explanation is that this long period of immaturity is merely a side effect of other developmental processes that must occur while we are young, delaying the transition to full maturity.

The most likely of these processes is the development of our brains.

While we humans have large and complex brains, they are not exceptional among primates, or even other big-brained animals. However, our cognitive abilities clearly distinguish us from other animals, and so it seems likely that something about our brain development, perhaps the degree to which neurons can be interconnected, or the "computational" complexities of particular regions of the brain, say, the cerebral cortex, or how different regions are interconnected, requires additional time during childhood.

Much of our brain development occurs after birth: there

is a limit for how big a newborn baby's head can be if the mother is to survive childbirth. At birth, a baby's brain is a quarter of the size it will be when that person matures into an adult. By the age of five, our brains are 90% developed, with the process only being completed in our early to mid-20s.

One explanation for why we need such complex cognitive/computational abilities is that during evolution, we quickly became our own worst enemies. That is, our most important and potentially dangerous competitors are ourselves, and some scientists have suggested we developed our big brains to analyze social interactions with other members of our species in a kind of cognitive "arms race," such that we can analyze and anticipate other people's actions before they take them, giving us a cognitive advantage in both cooperation and conflict.

Scientists have suggested that a long period of brain development extending human childhood may have become adaptive in and of itself, that is to say, this period of immaturity, which otherwise might be a detriment, has been "put to good use" by evolution. While facilitating brain development, it also allows plenty of time to play, encouraging the exploration and learning of social interactions. Childish overconfidence may encourage challenge-taking and learning by failure. And so on.

There is also evidence to suggest that trying to rush childhood can be counterproductive. Premature visual experience in birds can interfere with the development of the auditory system. Monkeys trained on a task later after birth were more effective at the task than monkeys trained earlier after birth. In humans, a related phenomenon is known as "hurried child syndrome," where a child's life is over-scheduled, often with an emphasis placed on academic achievement. Hurried child syndrome can be detrimental to social and emotional development, and, ironically, also to long-term academic achievement, suggesting childhood should not be rushed.

However, whether hurried or not, childhood of necessity must come to an end.

Part of this process is driven by the timed changes in our own bodies, which thrust us out of childhood and shove us unceremoniously into adolescence, whether or not we are ready for it, and thence adulthood. It is a process involving dramatic physical and mental changes that must be negotiated by both child and parent. It is a particularly sensitive period, where damage can be done if the adolescent is exposed to experiences he or she is not yet ready or able to cope with, an acute problem in this day and age of poorly regulated social media.

But, even if such hurdles can be effectively negotiated, and the child or adolescent be placed in an environment that nurtures caring, learning, and understanding, to what extent is the molding of a young person's personality into one that conforms with an adult worldview indoctrination and institutionalization?

Every culture has a particular way it feels children should be brought up, partly for the benefit of the child and partly for the perpetuation of that culture's values. Where these goals conflict, the child almost certainly will lose out, although it may not be possible to see this from within the culture that perpetuates such "maladaptive" behavior.

Perhaps this is the purpose of adolescent rebellion: to test the limits of the strictures being imposed upon the child, and measure them against the child's worldview so that the child can try to ascertain the "truth" of what s/he is being told or shown. Ultimately, every young person must find their own truth within the culture they are part of. This may necessitate rebelling against that culture and leading efforts to change how the culture works.

Certainly, we live in times where young people must look carefully at the world around them and decide what they believe is fit for purpose, and what is not, where "fit for purpose" is simply the guarantee of a planet on which everyone has equal access to what we consider the basic necessities of life.

About The Author

The Thalidomide Kid

No ONE ever dared call him that in his presence. He would've kicked you to pieces if you had.

I can't remember his real name. Was it Ian? Something like that. Something simple, something unassuming, something that any mother and father would want to call their little son, newly emerged into the world, red-faced and crying, but in the Thalidomide Kid's case, with no arms, just little flipper hands emerging from his shoulders.

I never once used this nickname, but that's how I thought of him: The Thalidomide Kid. I was the new boy at the school. It felt as if everyone was staring at me. He looked perfectly normal in every respect. Only his arms were missing, like they'd been forgotten about. His hands were recognizable as hands, although they, too, were subtly deformed, but not so much that he couldn't hold a pen. All his clothes were sleeveless: his shirts, his sweaters, his jacket, his coat, everything. There was no need for sleeves.

I had never seen a victim of the Thalidomide scandal before. I had never heard of thalidomide. I was simply trying to cope with being newly arrived at the school.

My dad was a pilot. He started his flying career in the RAF, then worked for various commercial airlines, and, as a result, we rarely stayed in one place for more than a year or two. I was sent to whichever government school was closest to home; thus, I had to adapt to being the perennial new boy.

I must've been 14 when I arrived at the school with the Thalidomide Kid.

Fourteen is a bad age to change schools. Gone are the carefree days of childhood, when making friends was as easy and as frequent as falling over and scraping your knees. For pre-adolescent boys, the shifting of alliances was like the weather, changing all the time. One day you might be friends, and the next day enemies, but the day after that you would be friends again.

Once puberty set in, everything changed.

Adolescent boys, like dogs, mark and protect their territories, both in the little village where we lived and, more importantly, in the playground at school.

Some boys suddenly become substantially taller, heavier, broader in the shoulder, more muscular, and hairier than their compatriots. The rest of us share an unspoken understanding that this is a dominance signal, a physical manifestation of the need to compete for resources and, critically, access to females, instincts bred into us across millions of years of evolution. I had, as part of this transition, become increasingly conscious of girls, and the way they looked different as, apparently overnight, they were transformed into young women. At the same time, I became painfully conscious of the way I looked — gawky, pale, undersized, and spotty.

I was small for my age, but that made me light and nimble on my feet. I had already learned at previous schools that the best way to deal with bullies was to run away and hide whenever possible. However, effective hiding requires a knowledge of your environment. And I was in yet another new school, about which I knew very little and, most particularly, the best places to hide.

However, I knew I could rely on the school library.

The adults in most schools considered the library a repository of knowledge and a quiet place to work; therefore, they encouraged pupils to use it as much as possible, access being unrestricted during the school day.

For me, the library was primarily a sanctuary. It was a place where an adult was always in attendance, and therefore, the chances of attack were minimized. This new school library was the same — it was open all day, and, critically, during the break periods.

Hiding in libraries encouraged my reading habit.

What else was there to do in the library other than stare out of the window, and even I couldn't maintain that for long. I gravitated towards escapist literature because that is what I wanted to do: escape from the situation I find myself trapped in. And so, liking my science lessons more than any of the other classes, because facts were controlled by logic and not whim, I gravitated towards science fiction.

Of note, the library did not open until after the morning assembly — it was closed when we first arrived at school.

Living in an outlying village, I was ferried to school in one of a fleet of local buses that dropped us at the main gate every day. We had to wait on the playground until the classrooms were opened when the first bell of the day rang throughout the school. My bus was almost invariably the first to arrive, so we had the longest wait, while the other buses arrived and the playground gradually filled with students.

This enforced period on the playground was, for me, a stressful time.

Being new, I had no territory on which to stand. I had to watch everyone around me to see how they grouped themselves, to understand who owned which part of the play-ground and, therefore, where I might fit myself in. I was also aware that there were no teachers in attendance at this time, technically before the school day formally commenced — the playground was unmonitored, making it imperative to iden-tify who the school bullies were, because, having attended several schools by this point, I knew that every school has its bullies.

As in the other schools I had attended, the youngest students, and most particularly the young boys, would roam freely around the playground, often playing a game of free-form soccer with a ragged tennis ball, or chasing each other in a playground-wide game of tag, while whooping and hollering with glee. The younger girls and older students collected in small groups, claiming their territory by placing their school bags on the ground at their feet.

Initially, I stood by the wall near the entrance to the main school building, a position that provided me with access to the school office should I need to take shelter there. I chose an angle in the wall, which partially shielded me from students entering the playground, allowing me to observe them as they passed.

I tried to appear as casual as possible. I could not afford to seem to hide, because that would attract attention. I had already been tested by a cohort of younger boys, who gath-ered around to bait me. They lost interest when I did not react. I had to appear self-assured, casual, and apparently uninterested in everyone else. This was something of a chal-lenge, given that I had to follow what everyone else was doing to identify a safe place for myself.

Another rite of passage on the first day of a new school involved finding a desk in the form room I'd been assigned to. I was obliged to stand by the door and wait to choose a desk once everybody else was seated. As the other students became aware of my presence, standing awkwardly at the door, they would stare, more or less overtly, and whisper among themselves. I had no choice but to endure this attention, desperately trying to suppress the blush spreading across my face. Luckily, there were several vacant seats to choose from. I picked a desk at the back of the class, where I might surreptitiously watch my classmates without them easily watching me.

There followed, of necessity, the obligatory and highly embarrassing introduction during the morning roll-call. The teacher, reading down the list of students, called out their names, receiving a response of "Here," "Sir," or "Here, sir." I sat, my stomach tense with anxiety and my teeth gritted, while the other students sneaked glances at me. Coming to the end of the list, and detecting the little charge of excitement and anticipation in the air, the teacher looked up and saw me. I was the only new student in our class, indeed, in the entire fourth year (as the 14- and 15-year-olds were then known) and, as far as I knew, in the whole school. When I was asked to stand and state my name, and saw every head in the classroom turn to gawk openly at me, with expressions of amusement and genuine or malicious curiosity on their faces, I could not hide the trembling in my voice.

Form rooms at this school were populated with students of mixed academic ability. Students were "streamed" into A-, B-, or C-streams. As a new student who had arrived after the beginning of the Autumn term, I was initially placed in the B-stream, for want of any information about my academic capabilities. I would be moved up to the A-stream if I proved to be better than average, or down to the C-stream if worse.

The Thalidomide Kid was in my form room. He was certainly a C-stream student. Although the C-stream was nominally for below-average students, the stream was mostly populated with students who had no interest in the kind of learning offered at school. There were many such students at this school, which served several small rural towns and villages in a predominantly farming region, where academic achieve-ment was neither much valued nor of much practical use.

I found it difficult not to stare at the Thalidomide Kid. I could see that he did not want to be at school. He also inhab-ited the back of the classroom, although in his case, it was a matter of choice rather than expediency. In every way other than his arms, he looked normal. (The subtle deformities of his hands only became noticeable on prolonged observation.) He had dark, almost black hair, dark eyebrows, dark eyes, and a thin, narrow face that might have been handsome if he hadn't been sneering whenever he was around his friends or was conscious of being watched. His constant scanning of the people around him gave him a shifty, untrustworthy expression.

Every student was required to wear a school uniform. Only the Thalidomide Kid did not. He wore a faded jean jacket with the arms cut off, and drainpipe trousers that were short in the leg, to show off his boots — brown leather Doc Martens that laced up above the ankles. He walked with a swagger and a swing of his legs to draw attention to his boots. The only people I knew of who wore Doc Martens boots laced up above the ankles were skinheads. Skinheads carried knives, went around in gangs, and fought the police.

The Thalidomide Kid hung out with a coterie of friends on the playground, although I could tell that "friends" was too strong a word for the group he'd fallen in with. The group was led by the principal bully in the school, a boy whose name I have expunged from my memory. I'll call him Eddie for the sake of this narrative.

Eddie's position as school bully rested on the reputation of his older brothers, who had also been part of the student body but had left at the first opportunity (16 years of age in those days). Everyone in Eddie's gang was in the C-stream. It quickly became apparent that the purpose of the C-stream classes was to prevent the C-stream students from damaging school property, each other, or the teachers. (Later, I was to realize how unfortunate this was for those C-stream students who wanted to learn.)

Eddie's playground territory was by the gymnasium, far from where I stood by the main school building. I guessed they chose this location so they could slip around the back of the gym to smoke cigarettes. Eddie and a couple of his gang members caught the same bus as I did in the morning, and I knew them as the students who sat at the very back of the bus, secretly smoking or ogling pornographic magazines, and then boasting about it when the bus driver yelled at them to stop whatever it was they were doing. I was curious to observe how students segregated themselves on the bus, partitioning themselves by age, with the youngest nearest the front and the older students towards the back. Eddie broke this rule. He was not the oldest student on the bus. Nonetheless, he had decided he was king, and when he wasn't smoking or ogling pornographic magazines, he sat in the middle of the back seat, so he could see down the central aisle of the bus, surveying his kingdom.

Eddie and the other members of his gang seemed to have an ambivalent relationship with the Thalidomide Kid. I watched them carefully when I was forced to be in close prox-imity to them, as when we had to troop over to the assembly hall in the morning, or had to stay indoors, in our form rooms or the corridors, stairwell, and locker areas of the school buildings during break when it was raining hard or bitterly cold. This interest was not motivated by curiosity; it was a matter of self-preservation. I did not want to be where they were, but if I was forced to be near them, I wanted to be as inconspicuous as possible, ready to flee the moment the trouble started.

Still, my interest revealed that in the presence of the other gang members, the Thalidomide Kid often tried to assert himself, speaking loudly and acting with bravado, while the

others tended to ignore him. When they did pay him attention, it was often to belittle him. Sometimes they picked on
him, especially Eddie. Eddie would push and shove him
around, understanding that it was difficult for the Thalidomide Kid to balance without the use of his arms.

The Thalidomide Kid seemed to tolerate this as part of
the cost of being a member of Eddie's gang. He whined and
complained, but did not confront Eddie or the other
members. I believed I understood why he did this: to be on
the other side, outside of Eddie's gang, would've made him an
obvious and immediate victim, because, like all such gangs,
they preyed on the vulnerable and weak.

However, it wasn't sufficient simply to hang around in the
playground with Eddie's gang. Gang members had to be a
useful part of the group, to provide some asset that made
Eddie and the gang stronger, more respected in the playground, and a more interesting group to be a part of. Eddie
didn't tolerate the Thalidomide Kid as an act of charity. Far
from it. Part of the Thalidomide Kid's role seemed to be as
clown — they certainly encouraged him to clown around for
their amusement. However, the principal method by which
the Thalidomide Kid staked his claim to be in the gang was
through violence.

THE FOURTH FORMERS, my age group, occupied a building
separate from the main school building. It was a square, ugly
1960s structure with four classrooms divided between two
levels. There was a short corridor on each floor, a staircase,
and a locker area in the lower corridor. Although we were
supposed to be in our classrooms during inclement weather,
friends from different forms would move from classroom to
classroom, or congregate in the corridor, or on or under the
stairs.

Early on, when the rain beat down outside and I was still friendless, I would sit at my desk in my form room during break in the presence of a few other students, while the rest clustered together in knots, chatting noisily in the corridors. Sometimes, the Thalidomide kid would be sitting at his desk, two away from mine and close enough that I could watch him surreptitiously while he was on his own. He would take a pen in his deformed hand, lean forward close to the desk, and twist to one side, so he could write in an exercise book. He would have to swivel his head around by 90° to see what he was doing, his left ear almost touching the exercise book.

I didn't dare approach him or ask him what he was writing or drawing, but I was very curious to know. On these occasions, he seemed very different from the person he was when surrounded by other students or in the presence of Eddie and his gang. He was quiet, a look of intense concentration on his face, working hard on something in the exercise book, fully absorbed in whatever he was doing, as if the rest of the world no longer existed. I was fascinated by the way he held the pen in his fingers and how his hand articulated directly from his shoulder, and how he had to bend the wrist forward to reach the paper, and how he had to lay his head on the desk to work in this way, and how he would sit upright and flex his back, as if his muscles were giving him discomfort.

I was sure he was drawing, but I couldn't see precisely what he was drawing. From my position, two desks away to his left, it looked like scribbles. I wanted to ask him what it felt like to be him. I wanted to empathize, to sympathize, to understand what it was like to live with such a profound deformity. But I couldn't. I didn't know how to approach him or the subject without giving offense, rousing his anger, and risking a kicking from those skinhead boots..

As soon as the bell jangled outside the classroom to announce the end of break, we had five minutes before the lesson bell would ring. The spell would be broken; there was no time to say hello or comment on his drawing because, in those five minutes, we had to get to our bags from the lockers and scoot across the rain-slick playground to find our next class, which might involve trekking from one side of the school to the other.

Several girls hung around with Eddie and his gang.

They distinguished themselves by wearing makeup, tight blouses and skirts, and they flirted with Eddie and other members of the gang. They never flirted with the Thalido-mide Kid. Perhaps they hung around with Eddie to get access to cigarettes and to smoke at the back of the gymnasium. In my first week, one of them came up to me and grabbed me by the crotch. I was too shocked to say or do anything, and her friends collapsed into peals of laughter, presumably at the expression on my face.

Eddie had to place me in the pecking order within the school, and he did so soon after my arrival. He confronted me by the lockers outside my form room, shoving me and trying to trip me over. I stayed on my feet, knowing I'd be much more vulnerable to an attack on the ground. He swore at me and tried to provoke me into a fight, punching me in the chest and spitting on me. However, I was prepared to endure his attentions and the sneers of his gang, taking the first opportu-nity to break away from them, hide in the library, and then spend the next week there during each break period, until I was sure they had lost interest in me.

I FOUND a small coterie of friends simply through their proximity to the corner I had claimed on the playground as my own. There were six of them, students from my year, all of whom were, like me, in the B stream, and several of whom I shared classes with. This was a sufficient connection for me to sidle up to them one day, holding my sports bag in my hand, hovering on the periphery of their group for several break periods, until one of them, a girl, turned to acknowledge my presence, allowing me to place my bag on the ground by my feet, and claim my permanent spot on the playground.

Three girls and three boys — with two "couples" among them. One couple acted as if they had been together for years. The boy of this "married" couple, Dicken [not his real name], was the first of our group to be targeted by the Thalidomide Kid. I don't know what prompted the interaction. I guessed that the Thalidomide Kid had some previous grievance against Dicken before I arrived at the school.

We were in our small group during a break period when the Thalidomide Kid appeared with Eddie and confronted Dicken. Everything happened quickly. One moment we were chatting and minding our own business, and the next the Thalidomide Kid was pushing his face into Dicken's face and calling him a c**t. Dicken chose not to stand down or back away. Instead, he made some sarcastic remark or other in reply, something like, "It takes one to know one." The Thalidomide Kid attacked Dicken immediately and without hesitation, kicking him with an intense, concentrated ferocity, causing Dicken to stagger and almost fall over before he had a chance to back away, out of range.

The noise and activity attracted the other members of Eddie's gang.

The Thalidomide Kid pursued Dicken, swinging kicks at him. Dicken made a move to fend off the Thalidomide Kid's Doc Martens-booted foot, causing him to wobble and nearly lose his balance, exposing his vulnerability to being toppled over, and he desisted in his attack.

Eddie had been watching with amusement. He said something derogatory to Dicken about trying to trip the Thalidomide Kid over. Dicken, who was grimacing in pain and bent over, rubbing his legs where he had been kicked, said something that sounded like a supplication, but he did not back down. Eddie seemed uninterested in pursuing the flight, and the gang as a whole lost interest and returned to their patch of the playground by the gymnasium. Dicken made a show of swearing at them and giving them the "V" sign, but only once they had their backs to us and were out of earshot in the noisy playground. He made a brave face of the situation, telling us next time he would "lay into that armless bastard." We knew he wouldn't, and we knew we wouldn't step in to help him in any future attack, either. He limped around for the rest of the day, consoled by his girlfriend-wife.

Now that I had seen what the Thalidomide Kid was capable of, I treated him with the utmost respect. I stayed out of his way, avoiding him in the classroom during rainy break periods, no longer interested in whatever his drawings might reveal of his inner world. He had behaved like a maniac, going berserk when he was kicking Dicken. How could you fight back against someone like that? Especially when he had no arms. I could fully understand why Dicken had not returned the Thalidomide Kid's attack. He was so vulnerable to simply being pushed over and, with no arms to protect himself, injuring himself from the fall alone. How could Dicken have justified such an action?

Of the other two boys in our playground group, one came from the same neighborhood as Eddie and his gang, and he seemed to know them, if not as friends, then at least as acquaintances, which seemed to remove him from their list of targets. The other boy was already immensely tall, towering over everybody else in the school. However, like many very tall people, he was a gentle giant. Even so, he was also targeted by the Thalidomide Kid. He had not taken the challenge seriously, and indeed, he was so tall, with such a long reach, that he could hold the Thalidomide Kid off and avoid his kicks, after the surprise of the first kick, with ease.

OUTSIDE OF SCHOOL, I saw little of my playground friends.

We had moved from one small village to another, and in this village, the few neighboring kids were younger than I. They had no interest in me, and I had no interest in them.

My sisters had gone to live with my mother and her boyfriend, and I stayed with my father and his girlfriend. This was a mistake, but so would've been going to live with my mother, and I was too young to leave home. I stayed out of the way of everyone, ensconced in my attic bedroom, listening to the cricket on a little transistor radio and scoring the matches in the margins of my school prayer book. We had no television, so when I wasn't scoring the cricket, I lived in the worlds of the books I was reading.

Dad's flying and our peripatetic lifestyle discouraged the formation of lasting friendships. What would be the point, when we would be moving again in a year or two? I didn't think about it like this; rather, I merely experienced the consequences of the way we lived. I would make connections, make friends, create emotional bonds, and then have them taken away again, whether or not I liked it.

This was fine with me; I could cope with the situation as long as I understood the ground rules and could adapt accordingly.

I learnt self-reliance.

My fellow students were more problematic. The rules in the world of children differ from those of adults.

The Thalidomide kid was a particular complication. He had gone from fascinating me to frightening me.

His mother must've taken the drug during her pregnancy, probably to treat morning sickness. The drug was available from 1958 to 1961 in the United Kingdom. Half of the roughly 2000 babies who suffered defects in the UK because of the drug died within a few months of birth. For me, as a

14-year-old trying to survive a new school, none of this would've been relevant, even if I'd known it.

Eddie's increased interest in me on our morning bus journeys was the first evidence that trouble was coming. He was already on the bus by the time it arrived in our village. He usually took no notice of me. I sat in the middle of the bus, not too close to the front, where the younger children sat, nor too close to the back, where I would fall into Eddie's domain of cigarette smoke and porn-induced sniggering.

However, latterly, he made a point of watching me take my seat from his position at the back of the bus. I made myself as small as possible, sitting by the window, my head pressed against the glass, watching the countryside slip by. I got off the bus quickly and hid myself among the other students on the playground, as far from the gymnasium as possible.

Then the weather turned, and the rain started.

Slow, steady, persistent rain.

English rain.

You might stand around in it for a short while and tolerate it, but not for long. It soaked through everything until you were cold and wet, and your sodden clothes would stick to your skin, the water threatening to seep through to your underwear.

In the fuggy warmth of the classroom, the rain brought on a particular psychological miasma, induced by an insidious, numbing boredom, which was equally impossible to resist. Even I, already a consummate loner, found it hard to maintain a positive state of mind during these extended periods of wet weather. The simplest tasks became onerous, the air seemed to thicken, and time seemed to slow to a crawl. The weather became our prison: the lack of freedom to go outside was oppressive, crushing the ability to think clearly or think at all. At school, it was as if we'd sunk below the ocean, and at home I would be drawn like a magnet to my attic bedroom window, sitting and staring mournfully at the murky, sodden landscape outside.

The mornings were grey and cold, and the playground slick and glassy with puddles, their surfaces pocked with the spatter of raindrops. Not even the hardiest of students stayed out in the rain on the playground. Everyone retreated into the school buildings as soon as they arrived, standing around in the corridors, or by the lockers, or in the stairwells, dripping wet and waiting for the teachers to emerge from their common room and unlock the doors to the form rooms.

In the fourth-form building, when our form room was locked, I would find a place under the stairwell, out of sight, hidden by the other groups of students hanging out there. On these occasions, Eddie and his gang did not venture behind the gymnasium to smoke. It was miserable outside, and they'd be easy to spot, even if they could keep their cigarettes dry.

Perhaps the lack of a morning smoke behind the gym contributed to Eddie's boredom and irritability.

As well hidden as I was, I wasn't that well hidden. There simply weren't that many places to hide first thing in the morning. I could have retreated to the main school building. But I had no legitimate reason to be there; I would've been among students from either the school years below or above me, none of whom I knew, and would've stood out like a sore thumb. I could have waited outside the school office, but that would have brought attention from the teachers or the administration staff. There was no way I could explain my situation to an adult.

Why not?

The threat Eddie represented was not a matter they could intervene in. Sure, they could've brought Eddie into the office with me and asked him about my concerns. He would've denied them, and I would've placed myself in even more jeopardy for being a telltale.

The library, that sanctuary of last resort, was locked until after assembly in the morning. The various toilets around the school were dangerous places in which to seek shelter. They had only one way in and out. Therefore, you could become trapped in a location that was both secluded and might not be patrolled by a teacher at all. Indeed, it was a nightmare of mine that, using the toilet of necessity, I would suffer just such an entrapment, with no way out that did not involve fighting.

I had a deep aversion to the idea of fighting because I knew the only way to win against Eddie and his gang would be to fight hard and fight to hurt. I was fully aware that such an approach would fuel a response in kind, and, being small and light, I did not rate my chances against Eddie himself, and it was highly likely that the other members of Eddie's gang would happily join in any attack on me.

And then there was the Thalidomide Kid.

———————

I SHOULD HAVE KNOWN the attack was coming because Eddie had walked up the aisle to my seat during the journey to school and punched me in the side of the head, such that I cracked my temple against the bus window. I was stunned by the blow, my ears ringing. He casually returned to his middle-seat throne at the back of the bus.

Once at school, Eddie made a point of following me from the bus across the rain-slicked playground to the fourth-form building. He shoved me as we walked and tried to trip me. I dodged his attempts. Perhaps this was a mistake. Falling over into one of the puddles and enduring a few kicks might've satisfied him. However, I wasn't thinking coolly and logically. I was panicked and afraid.

All the form rooms were locked inside the fourth-form building. Eddie was still following me, still shoving me as we entered the building. The other students saw what was happening and cleared a space around us. I backed away from Eddie until I came up against the lockers, holding my sports bag up in front of me for protection. He tried to punch me, and I used my elbow to deflect the blow. His fist hit the locker with a resounding bang. He kicked me and swore at me, demanding I hand over my sports bag. The bag contained my schoolbooks, sports kit, and a packed lunch. If I handed it over, he would take the contents out and scatter them across the wet playground. I didn't respond. He swung another punch at me, catching me square on the ear, and then grabbed the bag and tried to wrench it out of my hands. I held on tight, and when he relaxed his grip for a moment, I yanked it from him. Someone hissed that a teacher was coming. Eddie immediately backed away into the watching crowd.

The teacher, stepping into the foyer, didn't seem to notice anything unusual and proceeded to unlock the form rooms. Students filed into the classrooms. The teacher left to return to the common room. I took my place at my desk at the back of the class. I could see Eddie in the foyer. He was joined by several of his friends, and then by the Thalidomide Kid. They were between me and the exit. The class was half full. Most of the other students were clustered around the teacher's vacant desk. The windows were misted over with condensation on the inside and smeared with rain on the outside. I could see Eddie talking with the Thalidomide Kid and pointing at me.

I felt sick to my stomach.

The Thalidomide Kid stepped into the classroom. He stood by his desk, two away from mine. His desk was the closest desk to the classroom door. I tried not to look directly at him, but watched him from the corner of my eye. I could see Eddie in the doorway behind him.

The Thalidomide Kid said something to me. With my ear still ringing and feeling like it was swollen and puffed up into a mushroom on the side of my head, and my heart pounding like my ribcage was going to split open, I didn't hear what he said.

He repeated himself.

Eddie wanted my sports bag.

I shook my head.

The Thalidomide Kid pushed his way to where I sat, shoving over chairs and desks, and repeated the request: Eddie wanted my sports bag.

I could see Eddie turning his head and glancing back into the foyer, presumably keeping an eye out for the teacher. I looked up at the Thalidomide Kid. I wanted to implore him not to use violence. But he had to keep Eddie sweet. There was no way I could appeal to him. No reasoned argument I could present to him, no alternative course of action that would save my hide. So, I just looked at him.

In the doorway, Eddie said, Get a f**king move on.

The Thalidomide Kid swung a kick at me. The toe of his Doc Martin boot caught me in the shin, knocking my leg under the chair. I stood immediately, but not before he delivered two more kicks to my other shin and knee. I pulled my chair in front of me as a barrier. He used his foot to shove the chair out of the way. I held on, preventing him from doing so. He almost fell, swaying his body with an odd snake-like movement to prevent himself from toppling over. That was all it would take to stop him — make him fall over. Only, if he did, he had no way to protect himself from the upturned chairs and desks we were standing among. He could crack his head open.

Eddie was saying something in the doorway. I could see the girl who had groped me. She was smiling, enjoying the spectacle. The Thalidomide Kid was watching me through narrowed eyes, a cold, toothy grin on his face. He had good teeth. He couldn't get a clean kick at me while I stood behind the chair, so instead he leaned back and to one side, raising his foot and, using the sole of his boot, gave me a vicious karate kick to the thigh. I wasn't quick enough to avoid it. My leg went numb. I staggered and held onto the windowsill. I was petrified of falling over and becoming an easy target for his Doc Martens boots.

In the doorway, Eddie hissed, Get the bag.

The Thalidomide Kid looked bemused.

My sports bag had fallen over on the floor. He couldn't pick it up without kneeling down and almost kissing the ground in front of me.

There was a commotion in the foyer, and the teacher reappeared.

This time, he could not mistake what was going on. He marched into the classroom, ordered the other students out, closed the door behind them, and had me and the Thalidomide Kid stand in front of his desk while he gave us a talking-to about fighting in the classroom. We were both given a week's detention. Neither I nor the Thalidomide Kid said anything, because there was nothing to say. Later, I was asked to remain behind by the teacher and was given a lecture about fighting with people who could not fight back.

In the spring of that school year, Eddie and the Thalidomide Kid were both suspended from school for having attacked a student in the gymnasium changing rooms and knocking out two of his teeth. The rumor was that he'd been sitting down on the changing room benches, hadn't seen the Thalidomide Kid approaching. He'd been kicked in the face, swallowed his teeth, and had to be taken to hospital.

Although Eddie returned to the school and would occasionally bait me, he never again attacked me.

The Thalidomide Kid did not return. I never saw him again.

I can't imagine what it must have been like to have been a victim of the thalidomide tragedy as a teenage boy and have to face going to school every day of the week.

My 14-year-old self could only see Ian as the Thalidomide Kid. I never dared say those words in front of him, for fear of his reaction, or in front of any of the teachers, because they would have misunderstood. And anyway, there was never a need to name him because, apart from those first few occasions I watched him drawing, I soon learned I wanted nothing to do with him. And hadn't my nascent interest merely been voyeuristic? I am sure many other students at the school struggled with the same reaction. Ian must've known this. Perhaps this was part of the source of his pent-up anger.

Although it seemed to me he was trapped into siding with Eddie and his gang, purely as a matter of self-preservation, it might also have been that Eddie offered him a way of expressing his rage at the terrible injustice he had suffered and the attention he attracted because of it. I also suspect Eddie used Ian to achieve his violent ends for the simple reason that it was difficult to retaliate against someone with no arms, who was so vulnerable to the simplest of shoves.

While my friends and I ignored Ian as much as possible, and never once baited him because of his condition, nor did we show him any friendship, nor an alternative home to Eddie's gang. We didn't even step up to defend each other when we were attacked by Eddie or Ian. I suspect we all felt that ignoring Eddie and Ian and their exploits at school, and offering only passivity in the face of aggression, was the safest way to avoid conflict. Sure, we might individually get picked on, but we'd come away with nothing more than bruises, scrapes, and the temporary sting of humiliation.

On the other hand, this acquiescence to their violent behavior may have been what encouraged Eddie and Ian, and the rest of the gang, to attack the student in the gym and seriously injure him. If we had turned around and resisted, Eddie and Ian might have thought twice about attacking other students, and perhaps there would have been a different story for me to tell.

Guy Riddihough

RESOURCES

THE THALIDOMIDE TRUST, UK
    https://thalidomidetrust.org/about-us/about-thalido
mide/

THE THALIDOMIDE SCANDAL
    https://en.wikipedia.org/wiki/Thalidomide_scandal

THE SCIENCE MUSEUM, London
    https://www.sciencemuseum.org.uk/objects-and-stories/
medicine/thalidomide

THE GRÜNENTHAL COMPANY (MAKERS OF THALIDOMIDE)
    https://www.thalidomide-tragedy.com/en/the-history-of-
the-thalidomide-tragedy

The Four Ages of Death
BY GUY RIDDIHOUGH

A COLLECTION OF THREE NOVELLAS AND ONE NOVELETTE
FOUR DIMENSIONS OF THE FUTURE.

THE FOUR AGES OF DEATH—In a future where humans have spread across the Galaxy and lifespans can be extended for thousands of years, will life itself become an unbearable burden?

THE DAY IT SNOWED FOREVER — Would you be able to survive in the face of the extreme weather events that disrupt the modern-day infrastructure we take for granted?

THE IMMERSION CHAMBER — How far should we go to exert our moral authority in protecting our way of life from those groups we consider our enemies?

NOVEMBER SKY — You are responsible for judging the human race based on how we treat the people around us and the animals we use to better our lives. Do we pass? Or fail?

AVAILABLE FROM AMAZON AND BARNES & NOBLE

www.guyriddihough.com